ISBN:

# Destined Forever

VAISHNAVI.M

# DEDICATION

Dedicated to all of my readers who struggle with the confusion between friendship and love.

# ACKNOWLEDGMENTS

I would like to thank my family and friends who have supported me through this journey and encouraged me in all the ways they can.

# CHAPTER 1

With the bright light rays hitting directly on my face, I struggle to open my eyes. I know it's late but happy it is Sunday morning. Saturday night is always a time for us to sleep late and have fun on our way. Not sure if Stella is awake or not. I rolled over from the bed to the side of my table and picked up my phone which had a few messages and a missed call from her. Struggling to get up, I heard my mom singing in the kitchen and I could smell the yummy breakfast. My tummy turned into a knot out of hunger, so I hurried up to the bathroom and got freshened up quickly. Walking down the steps the music got louder with my mother's humming and fresh food was served at the dining table. I quickly take up a bite of the cherry red waffles which dissolve easily into my mouth. It was a delight and heavenly for my growling stomach. Also, there was my favourite pancake with banana and honey placed next to it. Inspecting everything I went near my mother and gave her a small hug.

I think until then she did not notice me or was completely involved in the songs playing over the speaker. It's always been only mom and me at home. Since dad is a businessman, he always keeps on travelling and comes home rarely once a quarter or something, and stays for only a few days. But he has not kept us in the absence of any needs like, setting up this speaker from the living room to the kitchen almost all over the house and making sure we get everything we need. whenever we ask him anything, apart from his physical presence everything gets fulfilled. My mom used to be proud that he bought this house immediately after their marriage with extra rooms planned even for children and he always takes care of the family. But I don't agree with it, because it always seems to me like he loves work more than his family and always gets busy in his office. Initially, he was working for a small start-up company and then later became the CEO of that company. I had very less time spending my childhood or the holidays with him. It's always been like a short movie or dream whenever we spend time with him, but yeah still he would try to do all the nice things in that short time and will get me all the kinds of stuff and things I wanted. But as I grew up, I always feel like our relationship is growing apart when he comes home, and I just have only a formal talk about the usual stuff and look after my work. Later it became I just talk to him only to ask things and vice versa. I have always been my mother's pet where I could share everything about whatever I felt, and she has always been like a mentor with so much support in my life. Before their marriage, they worked in the same company and fell in love which led to their marriage after that he was not ready to send her to a job that made her a housewife. At times she used to go out to buy things or groceries and her only pastime is this music or time spent with either me or Stella's family.

"So, what's your plan for today, Rob?" She turned her attention to me while I was stuffing food into my mouth and sat on the slab in the kitchen next to her.

"Do you ever use the table?" she scowled.

"It's not my kind of type mom" I say and pull her cheeks playfully. "What is your plan today mommy?" I gave a sarcastic smile.

She looked over at me and didn't answer my question" Stella was calling up. Hope you don't make her angry"

Talk of her and she arrives with her loud voice "It's always his habit to irritate me, so I don't bother it Mrs Richard".

I know it always bothers her, "Lier" and I winked at her.

She came up to me and hit me hard over my left shoulder and then caught up to the pancake which I was eating stuffing into her mouth.

"Do you want some Stella?"

"I would love to, but unfortunately my tummy is full" she answered and yet took a whole piece and had it for herself.

"Why aren't you ready still?" She showed me my pyjamas.

I gave a small knock on her head and pulled up her pony hair. She struggled and before she could hit me, I got down from the slab bowing up to her "At your service mam. Is there something I can do for you?" I taunt her.

She rolled her eyes and pushed me to stairs "Go get ready in 10 minutes or else I will have to do it by myself"

So dramatically, I leave them in the kitchen, hearing their gossip and giggles as I walk to my room and take the shower. I Wear my regular black jeans and a matching sweatshirt and make my way down the hallway. Stella, my one and only childhood friend sitting on a sofa with her leg crossed looking up at her phone. I always admire her way of dressing. She was wearing a black skirt with matchable stockings and an apt tank top for it having some wording printed covered by a black jacket. To be honest I'm also one of the reasons for her way of dressing since I chose most of her outfits. Looking up at me she showed her phone in her pocket and jumped to me holding my hand.

“See you later Mrs. Richard” and waved at my mother pulling me outside.

I just looked back giving a smile to my mom and we both almost ran out of our house.  After a few steps, she started to do her regular way of walking with jumps and turned her face toward me with a grin on it "I have the craziest plan for us".

“I bet it would always be the same plan” I muttered, and She gives me an irritated look and ignored me walking in her style.

“Since our graduation is going to happen in a few more months, I have to make myself ready for it and have lots of shopping and stuff to do. So, as usual, you are going to help me with it. Now Gotta say for your bet? It's going to be a complete shopping Sunday”.

“Why don't you plan with your other friends and make it a girl's day?”. I raise both of my fingers and make her gesture back “Girl's shopping Sunday”. Stella has more friends from her childhood and is always surrounded by people to whom she will talk so freely and make friends quickly. But I lack so much in that quality, I don’t go around with people much and am more of a lone type of guy exactly like my mom. She is my very and only best friend of mine. So even a day would not end without talking to her or meeting her. I have always loved the company of my own until I met her during school where She was very annoying yet a lovely friend to be with. We also ended up joining the same high school, and the same college and spending not just most but all our time together. She lives two streets away from my house and has lived in the same place from her childhood as me. We both also have a plan of sneaking out of this town and moving out after our graduation which is still a work in plan. Even though she has more friends, she always chooses me over everyone else which makes me proud of her and our friendship.

"You know only you can make me feel complete satisfaction. So better not try to escape from me, which you can't". There comes her mixed up of angry, emotional and terror face.

Just to make her happy and spend my time with her we finally agreed with each other and made our way past the shopping mall.

It's been more than three hours and we have gone through totally 5 shops by checking all the new stuff they had and yet have not finalised one. It's always tough for girls to finalise a thing, and mainly in dress it gets very hard. But in this case, it was not her fault and completely mine. I always choose and pick the perfect one until it gives me complete satisfaction, which still I have not achieved. And being my Stella, she is never tired of anything and the only result she needs is my selection. So, we spent nearly 6 hours of shopping and ended up purchasing not even a single dress for graduation. But we both have got other normal, casual, and usual stuff for both of us and after a long tiring day, we reach our favourite spot for dinner to a restaurant which is kind of a café shop.

With complete relaxation, we choose our favourite and all-time seat near the window keeping our shopping bags apart. We have always been a regular customer, and we never fail to come on every weekend. Or at least once a month where we sometimes visit during our weekdays as well. We spotted this shop a few years back and worked here part-time during our summer holidays. Since this shop is located on the corner of the busy street, from where we could see all the lighting and people passing by enjoying our meals with these beautiful eye fascinating views and it is also located near to both of our houses in the center of our small town. We always spend our time here and have loads and loads of lovely memories, which we never miss to speak of it every time.

“Welcome” the waiter gives his brightest smile “is it the same order or anything different.” We have always been his favourite customers. So, he does know our choice.

“It's the same”, I smile up at the waiter who has been nearly a friend to us and yet we keep forgetting his name.

We do our usual things, teasing each other, and talking about lots and lots of things while having our meal.

The main part of our fun is looking around hot girls and guys like choosing one for each other with a total zero percentage of interest. It's kind of fun which we started doing in our high school days. We would discuss this as if we are seriously choosing life partners for both of us. Stella has a fantasy dream of the love of her life and she used to tell that she believes in all this true love stuff and all. But I don’t feel any of it. I have never seen it in my life, all I have seen is achieving something in life is more than love, like my dad, concentrating only on his life and not on my mom. Whereas on the other side, my mom is so stupid and mad to always circle my dad, leaving her independent life for him in the name of love. She says that she trusts him completely and I call it blind trust, since I don’t see any of the efforts from his side. But I do respect my mother for her decisions and would always be there for her.

Still, all these make me not to believe in all those stuffs, but Stella in spite of having such an awful parent who doesn’t end up being together still believes in it. It always makes me shocked and also kind of angry at her. Because I don’t want her to end up stupid due to her fantasy of this love logic. She would always tell there would be her prince charming waiting for her with hearts and flowers. I wish she could be right when there are no such things in actual real life. As I support my mother, I do support Stella as well. And I don’t want both of the important ladies in my life to get hurt. So, I choose to be on her side when she chooses her perfect partner which has not happened yet and won't happen ever as per my knowledge. Because for me nobody is perfect in this world.

I would never have a conversation with Stella about this. It makes her upset whenever I tell her my point of view. And she would also not push me so much into this topic. Still, we enjoy talking about a few parts of other interests and love life. In spite of different thoughts, we still do enjoy our moments teasing things about it and when the conversation goes a bit serious, we would change it and bring back our fun mood. Finally, our day gets over by waving at each other with tired faces. I drop Stella at her home and reach my bed for a peaceful sleep..

# CHAPTER 2

Here we go again for a routine Monday which is always sick after having the weekends by going to classes. We live in a major city in Canada called Vancouver. But we don't live in the center of the city and are not too far from it. We live exactly in west point grey, having lovely neighbours and the best place for families. We could have many interactions and help needed whenever necessary. But I chose to be a self-contained person and so as my mom. So, we don't interact much with the neighbours for gossip or any other stuff.

To our college, we both always go together. Stella always gets ready and comes to my place and from there we would always get compact in my small car which is a Silver Toyota that should have been in red as per Stella's wish. But finally, I made it look classy and different from all others. Actually, it wasn't exactly silver in colour, but of the same family. Our ride to college would always be fun hearing our favourite songs and enjoying the beats of it which makes it even more enjoyable since both have similar tastes in music. We both are completely different and yet the same which proves in many things like one of our courses where I had no other choice than to choose international business due to my dad which further became my interest as well and Stella does

Interior Architecture since she has a creative mind and good designing including drawing skills. The only class we have in common is English. We both are very fond of it, but still different in our way of it. She likes to read more books and on the other hand, I like to watch only movies and series.

We reach our college, waving to each other in a hurry bye splitting up to our respective classes. Later we always meet during our lunch breaks and return home together. My classes were boring and were waiting for those to get over so I could go for my lunch. I am also interested in photography and I do some clicks in my first ever camera which was gifted by Stella on my 16th birthday. The pictures from my colleges are mostly taken during these lunch times, where I and Stella would always choose a different place each day and we once decided to make it a cycle for all five days in our week. Immediately after my teacher left the room finishing my third class of the day, I moved quickly for my lunchtime where in a hurry I suddenly got bumped by Leili who is also known from my high school. We three studied in the same school and ended up in the same college where in school she was the most popular and spoilt-up rich girl. She was the head cheerleader and has a huge crush on me and she hates Stella being around me. Due to this Stella never got an opportunity to join in cheerleading group, which in turn made her interested in sports and she was the captain of her game. Stella was also equally famous as Leili. So, it would always be a competition for her with Stella.

“Oops, Sorry handsome” is her usual way of overreacting and engaging me in her attention-getting playful or boisterous behaviour.

“It’s okay, I’m sorry” I replied and turned in the direction of reaching my place of destination.

“Where are you running? It’s lunchtime. Come let’s have lunch together. I could send away my friends, only for you”. She speaks out those words from her mouth full of red lipstick, in a flirty way and tries to get closer to me, winking her eyes. She always dresses up acting like a perfect model and does too much makeup which I don't like much and is not of my interest.

"Thanks, and I'm already having my date with me for my happy lunchtime. So, bye". I smile at her and waved moving out of that place. She knows exactly whom I'm referring to and I like to make her angry by mentioning Stella because she can do nothing about it. Moreover, she has tried many ways to bring up a fight between both of us during our school days, and gradually it got reduced in our college days. Maybe she got mature enough or she got tired of losing with both of us. Still, I don't like her character or attitude.

As I move to the garden, the colour of nature and its beauty captures my eyes and makes me fall for her and that is the main reason we love it to choose it as our Monday place. Also, it's our most favourite place and would spend more time here despite having other good places in our college. With the sound of the shutter click, I turn myself to see Stella taking pictures of me. She always does this as a habit of taking pics without my knowledge. Her interest in photography grew with me which wouldn't be professional yet she has a huge collection of photos, especially of mine saved in her album. I got her a small instax mini camera in my first part-time job salary which was very useful for her till now and at times gives me advice to improve my Photography skills as well.

"Look how cool it is" She showed the picture to me and to be honest yes it was a very good one. It was covering me with this beauty of nature at a perfect angle.

"This is going to be one of my favourites" I smiled and tried to take the picture from her.

She hides it behind her back with one hand “Never. It always belongs to my collection”.

We sit under the big tree and have our lunch sharing the conversations of our almost half day of classes. She is the talkative one and will never be out of topics to talk and I always am a good listener to her. But the good part is, no matter how much ever she talks, she also turns up to be a good listener when I speak or tell something. It goes up either way which is good for both of us.

As our day passes by with the usual boring classes, I wait for her in the parking lot which happens most of the time by her being late. She then comes with her class of girls walking by and waving byes to each other. Then she happens to cross a spoilt gang of guys in our college with its head as Sam, where each of the guys has dated almost all of the girls and yet still tries to flirt with Stella. With their dramatic taunts, they start teasing Stella which irritates her so much, and turned to anger by seeing me not helping her out, which I'm not good at all. Sam used to tell me he has real feelings for Stella and it's not one of his games but Who knows, this guy can never be trusted, and I will never let him near Stella at any cost.

Whatever, Stella being in her usual way, she is very strong and manages to find a way out and escapes from them or any other situation she faces.

During our drive back home, we stopped at a store to collect a few things needed for both of our houses.

“Do you know what is going on in college and the latest announcement?”

“Yes, I know”. Concentrating on my driving, I reply to her.

“Then why you did not bring it up till now?”

“I know you would eventually start with it since it is your favourite topic”. Yes, it is her favourite one, called Prom, which I have no interest in at all and because of me she hasn’t gone during our high school.

“Are you really not excited for the prom?”.

“Nah not. You know me well. I don't do the dance thing or hang out anywhere much”.

“Yeah, but this is our last prom as students, teenagers, or whatsoever. And don’t you wish to come with me?” She gives good stress at the word me, mentioning she wanted me to be in this prom with her. I have never been out to a party or prom or any of such activities held. The only thing I go to see is her game and that's only for her. I accompany her brother, so no one gets a chance to talk to me. Also, I’ll be safe from Leili as well since she would be busy with her cheering group.

“I bet Leili would die to take you to the prom” She taunts me with her wicked smile which makes me agitated.

“I think she is tired of trying upon me”. I keep my face straight and don’t look up at her. She is eating her mouthful of chips facing me and doing this talking stuff.

“Are you planning to take Sam as your date or what? To the fact since I'm not coming with you, who do you really take up with you? I am sure you are not planning to go alone?” I give her a mischievous smile and I know she is desperate to go.

“Hold on Rob, it's just too much of questions. And to give a single answer to all your questions, I'm still thinking of going or not. Anyways there are still five weeks for it. Who knows what will happen in the meantime?”.

I am shocked. “Are you serious? You are not planning to go to the Prom. You mean “The Prom” I taunt her sarcastically.

“I said I'm still deciding.” She rolled her eyes and turned towards the window.

She does this reaction only when she is being worried or upset or something which is disturbing her, and I have no idea what it would be or may be due to my irritation.

After a few turns over the road, I ask her “What's the matter?" Questioning her seemed to be hard for the first time in my life and she was in silence all the time which is out of her nature.

“Nothing” She just shrugs, still facing the window.

“Are you fine Stella?” I couldn’t control myself from being ignored by her.

“I’m fine”. “It's just I'm tired”. She immediately closes her eyes and pretends as if she is relaxing.

She is not fine, and I could know it also I'm lost with options to cheer her up. I feel like I'm completely lost by her ignorance. She has never and ever been like this to me. She always used to be chatter box or fight with me if I upset her and we would always sort it out together.

Our remaining journey to home went silent. She would spend a few moments in my home and head back to her home later. But this time it got different which made me sure that something is wrong and she is not fine.

“Could you drop me in my home? I kind of feel tired and need to rest”.

I had no idea how to respond to this sudden change, so I just replied with a numb voice “Fine”.

I’m sure she might have found that even I'm upset because of her reaction, but she acted like she never noticed it and just got out of the car taking her things walking away.

She didn't even wave or say anything and after a few steps from the car, she just turned over and gave a glance with a nodding smile and went to her house. It was so odd and different even though it felt a bit relaxing for me. I don't interact much with my mom and went directly to my room having early dinner, mentioning I had more homework and stuffs in order to not make my mom know that I'm sad or upset. My mind was filled with her unusual events, and she hasn't texted me or called till now.

After a long thought I called her up which she picked up after the second ring. Usually she does it in the first ring but I'm happy at least she picked it.

"Hey, what's up. Too busy?" I wait for her answer

After a long pause she replies "Yep, just house stuffs and preparing dinner"

"Oh, pity for your mom to have your food." I try to make a small humour and tease her to bring her back to normal.

But it doesn't work "Hope she gets used to it" was her normal reply.

We were silent for a minute, because I was not sure how to respond to her and my mind went blank. I was also scared to not talk to her about anything that would make her more upset. Without knowing the reason for her mood to be like this, I wasn't sure how to react.

"Hey Stella" I gave a pause for her to respond, but she didn't. "Do let me know if you need anything, you know I'm always there for you and you can count me on anything and anytime". This was the only thing I could tell her and make her speak out about what's happening or going inside her mind.

"Sure. I Gotta go, See you later".

Something is wrong and I hope I can make her fine.

The call ended, and I was lying on my bed staring at the wall, thinking about all the possibilities to make her normal where I ended up going to deep sleep.

# CHAPTER 3

Stella POV:

After all my chores and having dinner. I was waiting for my mom who always comes late, lying on the couch with the blanket over me and watching TV. I couldn't concentrate on the show playing by thinking of my day today which was super weird by bringing on the topic of prom to Rob. I know how hard it is for him to think of going to prom but still I always wish to be his partner in it so that we could win something together despite winning over many things during our school competitions and games. No matter how much we are connected by being close friends and he gives importance to me in many things, it always makes me feel like I'm just a normal person to him and he might easily lead his life without me, which I could never think of. All these overthinking clouded my mind and as time passed, I drifted into sleep out of tiredness and sadness.

"Wake up Stella, it's time and you are already late". I hear a voice and am not able to figure out if it's real or a dream, then I feel a sudden shaking and wake up abruptly.

“I'm up,” I say in a lazy voice looking at my mom with a blurred image and rubbing my eyes to make it clear. She is standing with both hands folded across her hip and looking at me. I think she was staring and then she started yelling at me that she had to do all the work alone and needed to get ready for her job. Even though I help her with so many things she finds out the few flaws left over and always keeps on shouting, so it got used for me. Ignoring all of it, I fold off the bed sheet from the couch and move to my room to get ready. When I looked at the time, I had only 30 mins left to go to college so I hurried up.

I quickly think of Rob. Will he leave me and go? Should I take up the bus or walk? So many questions popped up in my mind and I thought of calling him immediately. Then flashing back to yesterday evening's events, I decided to call his mom to get an update. She loves me more equally to Rob and always takes care of me no matter what.

“Happy morning Regan.”, I don't know what and how to ask her. Because I wanted to make sure that I should not make her upset by letting her know that we fought, eventually we always fight over small things and that too would be silly where we would always sort it out within a few minutes.

“Good day Stella. Did he miss to pick up” hearing these words my heart got a small crack, then she continued, “I think he would be in the shower because I woke him up 10 mins back. He was dozing off so badly” she gave a huge laugh.

Something made my heart feel good. Not sure if it's her laugh or her words' confirmation.

“Cool Regan, I will see you in a few minutes.” I tried to sound cheerful, and we ended the call. I hope she didn't get confused since I didn't mention the reason for my call.

I quickly get dressed in my regular black jeans and sweatshirt covering up with a black jacket. Ran down the stairs to check on my mom to see her before she leaves and exactly, and she was packing her things in her hand back to leave. Then she gave me a few instructions for the evening before leaving.

I have been alone many times in my home, and still, I'm not getting used to it despite four years of habit. My mom was always caring and would be so lovable and sometimes she is, but after her divorce, she has not been the same. Went through so much depression and problems in which I was also one of them and yet she is facing it all well. Our family times together have always gotten very less due to more responsibilities on our hands and I miss that. In spite of all these, she always made sure that I and Scott get everything best of what we wished for and is necessary for our life. She has been the superwoman in our family and is still finding ways for her own happiness as well as ours.

I finish the food quickly, shoving it into my mouth and leave for Rob's house which is a few minutes walk to the next street. By the time I reach their home Rob exactly came down the steps with his Ruffy hairstyle not properly combed which I always do it playfully and half tucked the shirt in jeans. He looks up at my face in a surprised manner and stands in the way like a statue. I move away from him and reach for his mom trying to help her in setting up the dining table which is almost done.

"Rob, did you forget? Today I have an appointment with the doctor."

I felt bad that she had to go alone. "Can I join you?"

"It's so sweet of you my dear" she pulled my cheeks in a sweet gesture "It's already been so long since I was not able to visit the clinic and only today I got their appointment in their busy schedule which is during your class hours. So, no problem, dear, I will manage"

"She always manages everything" Rob replied in a dull note looking at his plate.

"Also" she voiced out in an ordering manner "After the appointment, I'm going out with Stella's mom. We will be back for dinner. So, you better be at her home and help with dinner. Don't be a bother to her." She gives him a look for the last statement.

"Yes, mom understood. Let me know once the appointment is over and I will call you during my lunch hours." he watched me in an observing manner "I'm happy at least you have company after that". He keeps his look still on me while talking as if talking to me instead of his mom. I turned myself away from his look and went to the kitchen for chores.

He walks away, takes his bag and starts to get his car ready.

"See you in the Evening" I mentioned it to his mom, and she hugged me before I left.

As we take the road in silence, he keeps the radio on. Many times, we have our drive without talking and just listening to the music but this time it was different, and I hope it makes him feel the same too. I lean on the seat comfortably with one hand my forehead and watching outside the window. Suddenly he drove fast, maybe that's when he realised that we were late, so I didn't give any reaction. The song was giving peace to my mind, and I got down from the car once we reached.

I met up with Kia and Jude on my way to class to go through the routine of our classes. During the lunch time once we were out of the class Ethan came running to us as we were about to leave.

With heavy breathing he stood there for a moment and opened his mouth "Finally we got the news"

I could guess what it was and got so happy.

“Yes, the tournament is on” he smiled

Both Kia and Jude also got excited. We three looked at each other with a huge smile and cheered, hugging and jumping together.

“This time it is going to be our game” Kia said with her hand fist. I gave her an agreeing smile and told myself, yes this is going to be the last match in my college and I immediately turned away running in excitement to our lunch place to meet Rob.

The time I reached the place Rob was not there and it was kind of a surprise for him to be late. So, I just sat over there and started observing the surroundings where I saw two birds playing with each other taunt fully. I wanted to capture those moments so, I took out my camera and started taking pictures of it where I suddenly got a breathing sensation near my ear lobe.

“Would you not take a picture of this beautiful model?”. I immediately recognised him but did not turn around.

I kept smiling, focusing on my current work and answered, “I’m not interested” and giggled.

He pulled my hand turning towards him and the distance got closed between us. I looked into his blue eyes which had a serious look and he mentioned.

“Are you really not interested in capturing me?”. I kind of felt his grip a bit hard and I could know for sure that he is not playing and is very serious about this question. But I haven't seen him this much serious for a small thing, where it always used to be me who reacts for small things like yesterday and that is when I got reminded of our conversation and pulled my hand gently from his grip.

Took my bag and got his lunch box placed in his hand “You forgot to pick it up in the morning” I tried to change the topic since I had no answer for the previous one. I also kind of felt like not answering it while having more confusion in my mind.

His mood immediately got changed and gave a huge smile" and that is why I've always got you.” he gave a pause collecting the box and sat at the empty place next to me “To always take care of me”

His charming smile and his good mood made me feel normal and I took my box sitting beside him. I was about to say” Do you know what?” and then immediately closed my mind thinking it's going the same as yesterday.

He gave me a questionable look, so before any thoughts get inside him and spoil our good mood, I tell him “This year's tournament is on” I tell him with a big smile on my face.

Splitting the food outside of his mouth he got cheerful and in a loud voice asked “Really”. I could sense he also got happier. Previously we were worried that we would miss this year's tournament since our college ends in two months, but hope we got lucky to have one in our hand.

“I hope I don’t get lost this time as well” I drop my face down, poking my food with the fork.

He placed him left hand over my hand with assuring comfort “This time you and your team are going to rock. I trust you”. His words gave me so much comfort and confidence in myself.

“So, I think today we will be having a meeting with coach and team and from tomorrow the practice begins” I inform him.

He casually eats his food asking "So?”

"Rob, you have to decide what to do for all of the evenings until the match. It's your call." Most of the time he would also spend time on the ground during my practice session which sometimes both of us get irritated due to Leili's presence, but apart from that he will always be there to support me. Yet this time I want to know what will he choose, the regular one or has he changed.

"I'd have to think only for today, since from tomorrow I could be in grounds with you". He was giving his thinking look after blurring out these words, which made me smile knowing he dint change after all and I was the one to be stupid to think him like that.

"Maybe I could go to the library today and lend some books to keep me packed for the rest of the days" he said and turned to look at me.

I just shrugged "As you wish my boy" and I had this feeling of a proud moment.

We finish the rest of our lunch and chat for a while until we know it's time for our next class then split up planning for the evening to meet up in the library. After completing my classes and packing all of my bags I joined Kia and Jude in our coach's room where most of the team members had already assembled and were waiting. Once the coach arrived and the remaining team formed, he announced a few of the details of rules and members' positions where he changed a few of them and also informed us that it might change in the course of practice based upon our performance. Also, he smiled at me and gave encouraging words with the final mention of Kia as vice-captain and myself as captain. All around us gave a cheering sound including the new members.

As we finished our meeting and moved out of the room, the cheering team came leading with Leili. She wantedly bumped into me and acted as if she didn't notice.

Jude stepped forward with anger to speak up, but I held her hand and signalled her not to waste our energy with them and we moved out. Jude is always the angry and brave person amongst our team who can never bear a single taunt and is always ready to fight.

“You should have let me speak Stella. These girls deserve some” she kept her face in anger mode.

“They are not that worth Kia” spoke Jude and I gave an approving nod to both of them.

Leaving them off to their work I leave for the library where I find it almost empty. I know it got late in our meeting but also know that Rob would have not left me. So, I go to our usual spot and find him resting his face on the table, placing the book above his head, and drooling. This scene made me laugh incredibly, but I tried to control it and move slowly toward him without making any noise. I took up a paper nearby and rolled it up round and tickled his nose using it.

He woke abruptly in shock and I burst out in laughter. He was searching all around like in shock of falling or something and it made me laugh even more. Later on, he noticed me and was looking with a blank expression.

“I didn't know you would be a sleepy head.” I laughed and sat in the opposite chair facing him and took the book which he was reading. It was Pride and Prejudice which he always likes, not because of the love in it, but because of Elizabeth’s character

“How many times would you read it?” I raise a question to him.

He shakes his head and wipes his face with his kerchief coming back to the real world, I think. So, I tease him back “Hope you weren’t dreaming yourself as Darcy” I giggle. Sometimes I feel yes, he is kind of Darcy type where one could never understand him at all.

“Good joke,” he says sarcastically and gets the book from my hand. “Can we leave” he stands up and gestures the way.

“Let me pick some books before we leave,” I say, making my move to lead him.

He bumps my shoulder from behind using his fists and I turn around to look at him puzzled

“I have already got it” she shows three books in his other hand shaking them.

It makes me happy when he does things needed for me without my knowledge.

With that happiness, we started our journey to my home and as usual stopped at the store to buy a few more things.

# CHAPTER 4

Rob POV:

We take all our bags and enter the house. Scott, Stella's brother, was sitting on the sofa and watching TV. He is doing his high school in some other city since he is living with his dad. He is very thin and tall boy with brown messy hair covered all over his face. He is younger than me but is equal to my height. Stella's father is not at all a responsible person and is always the worst intaking care of a family. Her mother is not very good as a parent, but she is a good human being which could be considered. Speaking of Stella and Scott's relationship, Scott was very small and he did not have enough maturity to realise what was happening around him during the times of problems. He is very short tempered and would not know how to handle things or decide what to do. It's the best thing that he listens to his elder sister and would always have an opinion of her in each and everything. Due to the situations they both also had to be in separate houses. Initially it was very hard for Scott, so many times he would just run away and come to Stella. But as days passed, he somehow managed and would come twice in a month and only during weekends. So, it was odd to see him during weekdays but also happy on the same side.

“When did you come here?”. Stella asks him and keeps all the things in the living room.

Stella's house is not big as mine but they have a neat and compact house which is perfect for both mother and daughter.

“I just wanted to see you both, so I came.” He said casually.

I and Stella exchanged a look. We definitely know there will be some problem. Because Scott wouldn’t just come by himself, even though if he had come, he would have rushed to his sister in happiness but he was still sitting on the sofa in the same place.

Stella has always been responsible, because from her childhood they have always seen their parents' fighting even after they got divorce. Sometimes Stella would bring Scott and come over to our home. My mother would always welcome them wholeheartedly. I have not spent much time in their house apart from a few weekends so, it always makes me feel a little bit odd whenever I reach their place.

Stella sits next to Scott and talks. I acted like I was ignoring them and was arranging the things in the kitchen which we got from the store, but still, I could hear their voices.

“Is everything okay?”

“You know the answer then why do you ask it and make things harder” Scott’s voice was a little shaky.

“Okay. We don’t have to talk about it now. Don’t you have school tomorrow?”.

“I could go from here if you’d wish” He was so careful in his response.

“Only until this weekend and you have to leave before Monday. Is that fine”.

To break their non-happy conversation, I take up two packets of chips and make my way towards them in the living room. without making them aware I jump up on the sofa next to Scott and Stella gives a jerk.

“Have it Scott.” I give him one pack.

“You are always my lifesaver.” He gives his cutest smile and leans over me stretching his legs over the table in a relaxed manner.

“So, who am I then?” Stella teases her brother.

“My life saver’s only friend”. He mentions it proudly and winks at me.

“And my friend dont care to have a chips bag for me” Stella throws a small pillow on me which makes the chips fall down.

“For god's sake stella” I turned over to the floor to check the chips packet and was happy to see that nothing had fallen down. I teased her back showing my pack again.

She rumbles through her breath and moves to the kitchen. I know definitely she is going to call me for help and which she does in the next 30 mins breaking my conversation with Scott.

Scott switches off the TV and joins me to the kitchen. “I would like to join if you don’t mind.”

I pat his shoulder and we three were having funny conversations with laughs, teasing, working and making the kitchen even worse than before. We were making sushi which is Scott's favourite and also was making some bread and dessert. Stella is always fond of having dessert whenever she gets the chance and that is when we hear the doorbell ring.

“I’d go check on it”. I tell them and walk to the front door.

When I open the door, I see my mom and Stella's mom sharing a laugh. Stella's mom gives me a hug and they get inside together.

"So are the dinner ready guys?" My mom asked me.

"Where is Stella and Scott?"  Her mother raised the next question.

"I have the answer for both of yours" Stella takes a bowl following Scott and places them on the table.

Everyone takes their seat and we all talk about my mom's appointment and then their outing in the mall, which was funnier when they talked about a lady who was acting weird and mad when she fought with the salesperson for not accepting her offer whose validity had expired a month ago. It was nice to have a laugh until a call came to my mom's mobile. It was my father. She took the phone and excused everyone, then suddenly disappeared outside to talk with him. I was not concerned about why he had called but was concerned about my mom's action. Everybody was silent and then Scott started talking to distract me and yeah, I got so lost in it that I did not notice my mom's return.

After dinner, we all had our dessert in the living room still continuing our topics where Stella talked about her tournament plans and my sleeping in the library as well.

The next day morning I didn't ask anything about my mom about her last night's behaviour nor did she come up with anything., unless she announced herself that dad has got some loss in business and he won't be coming this weekend to home.

"It's the usual, do we have any other special news?" Yes, it is not new to me. He always does this and I stopped expecting him for any of the weekends.

"He is working for us, Son". My mom places her hand on my head.

I did not respond to anything because I didn't want to show my anger to her and hurt my mom. I just move her hand slowly and make my way to the living room.

“You did not complete your breakfast, Rob”. Her sadness is clear in her tone.

“I got late mom. See you in the evening. Bye”.

I pick up Stella and we head to college.

“Why does your face have a moody look?” Stella asks as she changes the song.

“Nothing new, as usual, my dad is not coming over the weekend” I just shrug and concentrate on my driving. The song playing in the speakers is one of our favourites. I knew Stella has kept this to make me feel better.

“oh”. She gives a sound.

I turn to see her face; she is into something and her face falls down. She looks dull too. I keep looking at her to make her know that she needs to give a good response.

“What? Why are you staring at me like this?”.

“I’m not staring Stella I'm just looking at you” I give her a stern response. I really need her to speak up. She should not know that she can speak anything to me and not just give answers only when I ask.

“Okay fine I will tell you. Just don’t make me do this every time. Instead, you could directly ask me, right?” She smiles and it changes my mood as well.

“You know we are not just passing by strangers for which you should give answers only for my question. This is not us”. She definitely knows and she needs to improve herself in this.

“It's just, hearing your statement made me change suddenly like that. And actually, I was about to tell you everything even without you asking me. You know I do things for a reason” She gives a typical justifying look. Yeah, she is right, she does have a reason for everything and we could never argue it to be right or wrong, it's always we can only have discussions on it. She has a rule of nothing is right or wrong in this world and it's all on the perspective we see through the situations.

“You said you were upset about your father, right? And here I am getting disturbed by my father’s arrival” she tells with a deep voice and I can realise the pain in her voice. She doesn’t like her father at all. For every daughter, it would be like their father to be a role model or a hero. It is like a universal fact and from her childhood, it has been the opposite for her. But her father always tells her that he cares for her so much, but those will be only in words and when the choice comes, he always is selfish and does things only for himself and not even for his own family. I wonder how their parents even get married and have such loving two children.

“This morning dad called me and asked about Scott, while talking he told me he would be visiting over this weekend since Scott is staying here. I couldn’t say anything, I'm not sure if I should get angry at Scott for this or at my dad or at myself” She keeps her hand on her head getting frustrated.

I just place my hand on her. She maintains the same position and doesn’t speak even a single word.

“Don't worry I will be with you over the weekend and we can manage. Just relax. Also, we have Scott with us. There is nothing we three can't handle”.

She makes her face straight to me “It’s not about his arrival. I have the first match over this weekend and if he comes, he will know about my tournament and would act as if he cares for me and would end up coming to my matches. Again" Her eyes went small and nearly to tears. "Even I didn't tell Scott about my matches to avoid my dad coming and" She stumbles with her words.

It is a very difficult situation. Her father would not come normal to the match, he would definitely be drinking and it would always end up creating a scene, like the previous every time it had happened whenever he came to match. He does not have a good name in this city, to be honest he has many enemies due to his habit. This will create a big problem for Stella.

"I will make sure he doesn't come to the match. Don't worry" I hold her hand. I should stand for her. This is important for her.

Her eyes bloomed with hope "How could you? I don't want you ending up in a fight with him" there was fear and care in her eyes for me.

"No. I won't do anything that you don't like. But I will handle it. You can concentrate only on the match and bring me the cup. Won't you do that for me" I give her a smile.

"Definitely I will. But" I stop her and give her an assuring look.

We didn't talk about it further. As of now I don't have any plan to stop him, but I definitely will come up with a plan to make things right.

# CHAPTER 5

Stella POV:

The rest of the days pass by our classes, with my daily practice and Rob sometimes spends time in the library in case he has more homework or stuff, and other times he works on his photographic collections since we thought it would be best to start working from now so he could plan something for future out of it, but all of the time he would exactly come ten minutes before my practice session gets over and we will head back home together. The day before the weekend Rob created several ways to plan and keep my dad out of the tournament topic in one point, he planned to make me and Scott stay in his home, but later on, we came to a conclusion that it would not work and Rob repeatedly made sure to me that he would never let me down making sure everything will be fine. I trust him and I know he can do it, but I was also worried about the fact that this would make him miss my first match yet he convinced me and promised me not to worry about anything.

Rob POV:

It’s the weekend and I wake up suddenly getting reminded of Stella. I get ready and pack up a few of my stuff heading down to the dining hall. I have to be with Stella before anything goes wrong and should make her sure of tomorrow's match without worrying or getting upset.

My mom was busy doing laundry.

“You are up early? Are you going anywhere?”. I start to have my breakfast and inform her about my plan.

“Um, actually I was planning to spend the weekend with Scott, I meant in Stella’s house. You see dad is also not coming, so I thought it would be nice to spend some time with Scott since he is here.” I don’t know what her reaction would be and I don’t want to give any suspicious thoughts to her.

“Yea it would be nice. Do you have anything else planned, or that’s it?”?

“Nice of you asking, since I would be spending my night and all the weekend there, I thought you and Stella’s mom could stay here for the night and have your weekend as well.”

Now she gets suspicion. How stupid I could be, throwing everything at a time. I should have taken it slowly. “So, it seems like everything is being planned already. Rob? What are you up to”? She gives her a mischievous look, doubting me.

“Mom, it's just normal planning for the weekend. It doesn't seem weird or odd to me.”

“Odd doesn’t seem to be covering my son. But I'm happy unless you three are happy and spending time together. I will inform Sarah about this and we will also make our plan.” She gives me a knowing smile. I always love my mom for being supportive.

I finish my breakfast soon and take my car stuffing all my things in the back and move to Stella's house. I ring the doorbell. Stella opens it and gets shocked by seeing my presence.

"Is it really you, being so early over here? Am I dreaming or something"? She acts like pinching herself.

I push her away and make myself inside. "What makes you think so. Shall I make you realize of the reality". I take the glass of water to pour on her. She understands immediately and gives a jerk. "It's you who has to clean up if you do it." She gives a warning look, which is kind of amusing and makes my mood good & playful with her.

"You are always understanding", I give up on my idea & give her an appreciation taking my seat on the couch.

"So, what is about all of this, the compliments and your good moods." She crosses her hand over her chest looking so confused by my actions. She is still in her pyjamas. I think I had been too early which was making her so surprised more than my visit.

"Try to take compliments sometimes Stella. Isn't it late for your practice"? I gesture to her playfully and try to change the topic.

"If you are being so concerned about it then you have to be here by early 4 in the morning and not by 6.30. Also, today we are having practice in the evening, not in the morning." She tells and comes near to me. "Better have a good update for a plan to work out" she winks mischievously.

It was like she caught me up in the moment and I tried to maintain a normal self. Scott comes out from his mother's room and he also gets shocked by seeing me.

"Hey Rob, you so early?". He gives a puzzled look, looking at his sister and back at me.

“Why is everyone complaining to me about being early instead of appreciating?” I give a dramatic gesture.

“No one ever complains you dear.” Stella’s mom takes a bowl in her hand and places it on the dining table. “Come sit with us”.

“You are always loving Sarah. My appetite is completely empty with my stomach growling.” I walk toward her and give her a gentle hug from behind. She laughs and hits me softly. “Your mom called me and told everything. So, stop acting like a hero.” She gives her beautiful smile.

“I don’t know how on earth she could be so fast. Technology is improving.” I take a slice from the bowl and have a taste of it. It is not good with tase but still could manage to swallow under my throat.

Stella looks at my reaction and giggles, “So, it's me who is not still updated with details.” She joins over the table.

“You could add me too.” Scott joins the dining table and sits next to me. He takes the bite of the sausage and gives a yum sound. It's weird how he feels it is tastiest. Sarah used to make good and delicious food before, but as days started to go on, she lost interest in many things, and cooking is one of them.

Watching her son enjoying the food, Sarah gets happy. Maybe this is the whole point that Scott wants, seeing his mom happy. It looks so good to see the happy family and then the thought of their father interrupts and destroys everything.

Stella helps her mom and sits opposite to me giving a questionable expression. I just give her a nod and she doesn’t say anything in an understanding gesture. She is always an understandable one.

We finish off our breakfast and I reach the living room relaxing on the sofa. Scott goes back to his room. Stella comes by and sits next to me whereas her mom is still doing the dishes.

“So, what are you up to?” Stella gives a stern speech in her voice.

I switch on the tv and raise the volume much enough to avoid others hearing our conversation. Stella patiently waits for my response. I smile still, eyes focused on TV, testing for Stella’s patience. She is good at it, doesn’t turn away from me or speaks anything back and keeps on waiting for my response. Finally, I give up and ask her as if I'm not knowing anything. “So What?”.

“Do you really Wanna do this Rob?”. She is so serious in her tone.

“What do you mean Stella?” I just try to make her mood better and try to be normal.

“You know what I'm asking about.”

“Okay fine. Yes, I know exactly what you are saying. Now fine and cool. Let the adults handle this”

She gives an exhaust reaction and I could clearly see she is upset. “Rob, I don’t want you to do anything about the part of my life in which nothing can be changed.”

“I’m not doing anything much Stella; I'm just spending some time with you guys. That’s it. It doesn’t seem anything different to me”.

“I clearly know you have put some stupid plan over your head and you are not making me aware of it. Aren't we supposed to be partners? That is what we are right. I hope you didn't forget that part of our life”. she is done with her patience and really very pissed up right now.

“Fine. I will jump directly to the part. When do you expect your dad to come?”

She is silent for a few seconds, but at the same time I could sense a little of relaxation in her movements. It's a good thing.

"Any time today before night" She still maintains her silent awkwardness. Looking down at her fingers shows that she is more nervous.

I turn towards her and take her face towards me to make her feel everything would be fine. "Then we will be in the house until he shows up and waits for him. Simple".

"How that is going to be simple. You know what will happen when he does."

I pause her sentence "I know. I'm here with you and we are partners right. So, trust me everything will go well".

She gets a bit relaxed then again bursts up a question immediately back to all of her nervous and upsetting things. "But I have practice in the evening, also I need you to tell me everything. I don't want you handling things alone. Let me be there for you as well" she grabs my hand in hers.

It makes me feel good and it has the same effect on her as well. "We will sort out for the evening later, but for now after lunch your mom will be leaving to my place and spend the rest of the weekend there and I'm going to be here with you for. Rest we can discuss after your practice session."

She opens up her mouth where I again stop her placing my fingers on her lips "As of now discussion is over. I need you to concentrate on your precious evening today. Everything else can wait." She nods and gives a big smile on face. It's nice to see her happy and I would do anything to keep her happy as always like this.

I turn my focus over the television and try to pick up a channel. She moves closer towards me and lays her head on my shoulder.

"Thank you. For being here with me." She whispers in a more polite way.

"That's what friends are for." I pat her head and we continue watching TV. It's a good start to the day.

Later Scott joins us in the living room and we start playing. It's good to have Xbox stuff to pass the time. I'm not good at playing, but still, I only choose to play over here and only with them. Stella could never beat me in the game, so she gives in and hands over the turbo to Scott.

"I will check on mom and help her with dishes." She gets up from the sofa next to me which is immediately occupied by Scott, like he was waiting for the moment and finally he has got to achieve it.

Scott has been more like a buddy to me, even though he is three years younger than me. I don't share any of my personal details with him, but still it's like we both have a good bond which would always be cherished.

The time flew by so fast and both of us had no idea how long we were playing. We played more rounds in each of which we had an equal part of victories. We were actually having a count during the beginning of the game, later getting deeper we lost the count and concentrated more on the winning part.

Stellas breaks our flow by interrupting.

"I'm going to head for practice. Just take care of home". She has changed her dress and is packing her bags for the field. I lost the game because of her distraction.

"You lost" Scott gives a happy jerk.

"Where is mom?" Scott questions his sister.

"Are you guys so dumb? She left an hour back to visit Rob's house" She gives a glare looking at me. I know I should have noticed it, since it was part of our plan. But I got diverted once the game got started.

Scott just gives an okay and keeps silent, not knowing how to proceed.

“I will ask my mom for an update” I informed Stella. But she is not satisfied. Maybe she is pissed up on me or both of us for being careless.

“So, how are you going? Can we accompany you” I ask her. Scott gives a shocking expression at me. I think he was planning to continue on with the game, but I wasn’t planning on anything anyway. This weekend was to keep Stella away from her father's problems and I should focus on that.

“Looks like someone got responsible” she just speaks as she is packing her things. She is definitely tense.

“I might call up on Katie to pick me up. You guys carry on.” She takes her bag, crossing up over her shoulder and moves to pick her phone. She had not done it yet and she might have expected me to join. How stupid I can be when that was the thing which should have been done.

I quickly get up from my place and reach her phone before she does. I succeeded in it. Seeing her phone in my hand she looks puzzled. Maybe she was not pissed, but definitely she is in a bad mood.

“I think it would not be necessary. I will come with you” I speak softly and enough for her to understand. She doesn’t say anything and keeps standing still.

“I also would like to join you both. If you guys don’t mind” Scott speaks from his side. Good thing he understood and didn't make it look as ugly situation as it is already.

She just shrugs “Fine then let's get moving.” She gives a huge smile and turns her back towards me.

Scott goes to his room to get ready.

I hold Stella's arm and pull her towards me “Don't tell me it was one of your mischievous ways to make us come with you”. She giggles and gives her cute smile.

“Of course, it is” she says and wraps my finger which is still in her arms. "I know you would find it when it is done”. She still keeps her happy face and grabs her phone from my other hand.

“After you both got up to the game, you guys completely got lost in it. But I was so tense that my father might show up anytime. I made up my patience and waited till mom leaves.” She explains everything in a cool tone. “Later it was time for my practice and I was thinking what to do. I can't leave you both at home deciding or not when he will show up and create a problem” she lets out a breath after her speech.

“There won't be any problem. I assure you. Not this time” I say with confidence.

Stella replies in a relaxed way. “I know Rob. I’m happy you are here with us and supporting me through this. But I just can't sit simply and let you handle everything. I have to work from my side too.”

She keeps her head down in a low tone and lets her frustration out.

“I’m tired of him. Every time. I won't let him affect me this time” She turns again to look at me. Straight into my eyes. She looks confident. I like Stella being this way.

“So, I came up with a plan of taking you two with me. In case if he shows up no one would be at home and the problem would be solved". She gives a proud reaction to herself. It really got in my mind to tease her reaction, but I passed on that thought and pushed myself into serious conversation.

"Hope everything goes well. Even if he arrives while we are at home, we can handle it. You don't have to worry about it." I give her an assuring look.

"Rob, I was about to ask. You mentioned you would be telling the plans later. I hope we don't make late in our discussion" as she speaks her face changes back to a sad reaction.

"As I promised, we can speak once the practice is done. Now I want my captain to rock the ground".

As we have our conversation Scott arrives in the living room and takes the car keys.

Stella scolds him "You are not driving". She tenses all her worried reactions over Scott. Pity guy, he had no clue of how to react. As usual he was stuck standing like a statue.

I smile and get the keys from him "Relax Stella. He was just going to give it back to me."

"Sorry Scott" Stella gives her apologetical reply and moves towards the front door leaving both of us standing.

We both give each other a look and I put my hands over Scott to comfort him as we step out of the house.

# CHAPTER 6

Our drive to the ground was not very conversational. Each of us was filled with our own thoughts and Stella would be top ranking in those. I completely focused on her and the thoughts going inside her head which could be easily read from her face. Scott was making himself occupied by controlling the radio. It's upsetting to see her worried and sad. I look up at her each time through the mirror, since she is held in the back seat. She is deep into her thoughts looking over the window. Lately she was so happy about this tournament and now it has become her upsetting thoughts.

We reach the destination and Stella picks up her bag going to her changing room, informing us to be occupied.

“Is she fine?" Scott questions once we both get out of the car. He has always been a caring brother, but also, he is not strong enough to handle things properly yet.

“Everything is fine Scott. There is nothing to be worried about. Why do you think so?” I talk so casually to him.

“I know my dad is planning to come here and I know what happens every time whenever he arrives, especially during Stell’s tournament days." His voice tumbles and he gives a small pause for each and every word he speaks. I let him speak and observe his thoughts.

"I tried so hard for him not to come. I couldn't stop. Maybe I should have not decided to come here either, else we would have not been in this situation.`` He looked so sad and the frown on his face grew bigger than before. Poor Scott, this has nothing to do with him.

"It's not like that, Scott. You are always welcomed here. Don't blame yourself for things that you are not responsible of" I pat him on his shoulder and could sense his relaxation gesture.

"Do you really think like that? Isn't there anything I can do?" he gives a clear statement as if providing a confirmation that he is ready to do anything. Yes, I know he would do anything for his sister. Even though he is not mature enough to handle situations on his own, he always tries to stand up for his sister.

"There is something you can do," I tell him, giving him a smile.

He jumps exactly like Stella, like a child seeing a candy "Tell me what it is". I laugh loudly at his reaction and he still keeps waiting to get his candy.

I managed my humour and pulled him toward me hugging him over neck with my big arm around his small boyish face "Let's go cheer our captain". He gets in a good mood and gives a smile back.

We both walk towards the pantry area and get some stuff for us to eat with Scott's both hands filled up. We take up the third-row centre seat to have a good view of the practise session. There is not much audience, only 5 to 6 members are seated and watching the games. Who would end up on a weekend in ground, especially on Saturday where all would be in some house parties. Stella is giving instruction to her team as her coach guides everyone. It's a good evening to spend like this.

The practice match hits up the break and Stella looks around and gives a smile finding us.

"It's nice to see you both here" I hear a voice near me, making me jerk. It's Leili, giving her huge flirty smile towards me, accompanied by two of her friends on either side. Why do these girls always stick to her both sides like glue? I just give her a nod and focus my attention back to the field.

"So, what's your plan over the weekend?" In spite of understanding my ignorance, still she tries to have a conversation with me. Scott does not even give an acknowledgement of the girls standing beside us and keeps eating his popcorn watching the group in the field. I thought he would help me with something.

"Nothing much, just going to spend time with them." and I gesture over Scott and to Stella. That is when I notice Stella is looking over at us. I could not find any expression from her face, not sure whether it is due to the long distance that she is standing or she is not having any such expression at all. After a few seconds she turns to her bag and wipes her sweaty face, drinking her water and sitting up in a relaxing way. Maybe she just looked over and nothing more than that at all.

"So silly of you Rob. Why do you want to have such a boring Saturday night when you could come with me to the party"? Seriously, Leili asked me to a party which I have never shown up at all in my whole life. She keeps continuing with her words "Sam is throwing up a part for the tournament, so everyone is invited. Including the players and the cheerleaders" She gives a mischievous look and gets a bit closer to me.

I shift a bit away from her and towards Scott. Hearing her even Scott gets distracted which makes him gulp over his drink. "I'm not coming Leili. I have my plans." I just answer her in a normal tone, making sure of not giving any hint of my reaction to her.

"You won't even if Stella comes over" She raises her one eyebrow, giving me a challenging look. Definitely Stella would never go to a party, especially not to Sam's house party. She has also never shown up to any of those stupid parties, but she has gone to few small group parties with 5 to 6 members, which she describes it as a hangout and that is also only during special occasions like birthday, celebrations and so on. It's also a countable one, since she never drinks and has self-control. She would also ask me every time to accompany her, but I always refuse and I never have controlled her not to go. Because I know her, she can be in her limits and she has proved it several times. So, there is no way I could trust these words of Leili and have any suspicious thoughts about my friend. No matter how hard she tries to put it over my brain.

"If you have not heard properly Leili, it's Stella's plan with me for this weekend. So don't try to bring any unwanted conversations." my tone got a bit angrier and tensed. I know Stella, but I don't like Leili talking like this about her and trying to put wrong thoughts in my mind. It will definitely not work.

She gives her dramatic laugh, followed by the other two girls beside her. "You might not know. Anything might change at any time." she speaks over her laugh and continues "You could ask Stella, if you want and let me know if you are coming. I will always be waiting for you. Always".

She gives a pressure in each of her words and once her words are done, she leaves the place with her girls. It's a great relief that she has gone. I could not tolerate her more than this.

Scott doesn't speak anything about this and during the rest of the game he never brought about this conversation and kept talking about the normal stuff of the game and their way of playing. It was easy for my mind to get back to normal and I joined him along with his conversations enjoying the rest of the game.

It got dark and the game also got over. Stella and her team went to the changing room and we both made our way to the entrance of the ground, waiting for Stella to come up.

After 20 to 30 minutes Stella comes with her bag hanging over her shoulder and waving back to her teammates. There were a few conversations about the party when the girls' group was passing over us. I ignore it and turn my attention towards her. "So how was our game? Hope you both had a good time". Stella hands over the bag to me. I know she is tired.

“It was a good one. But the captain needs to concentrate more on the game” Scott teases her and they both give a playful hit to each other as we walk to the parking lot.

“I’m so hungry, can we have something before going home?” Stella suggested, looking over to me.

I just give her a smile and nod with her.

During the drive I did not speak anything, but as usual Stella was telling each and every detail of her session to both of us, even though we have watched over all of it. Scott teases her whenever he gets chance and they both do their happy and funny conversations. This time both of them were sitting on the back seat and I was left alone in the front driving. But it's nice to see them both tension free and spending some good time which did not make me feel alone. I enjoy their conversation even though I'm not involved in it, maybe that’s why I was quite though the whole time. I don't want to interrupt their sister brother's time.

I pulled into the restaurant parking lot and stopped the car. That is the only point when Stella and Scott give a pause to their conversation and look around. When I tried to see Stella through the mirror before they could get down, she looked back at me with her cute smile and got out of the car. I shut off the engine and came out of the car following both of them to the restaurant.

We take up a four-seater space, Stella and Scott sitting at one side and I'm on the opposite one. I could see Stella took a minute to decide which side to be seated which did not bother me by her choice. Since It's obviously known that still they both are in the same mood of the conversations they had during the drive.

The waiter came to give the menu card and each of us decided to give away our order. This restaurant is not a big one, just a small compact one with no rush. It is also a decent one with good food. This is not always our preferred place, but we have visited a few times and it's not a bad option to choose.

“I thought of planning up our remaining Saturday night and have fun” Scott says looking at me, then continues “If you are not tired” turning up to stella.

“Actually, I'm going directly to my bed once I reach home” she gives a dramatic yawn and moves her body in a stretching manner and then she laughs looking at her brother’s face.

“Kidding Scott. I would love to spend time with you both instead of wasting up a Saturday night sleeping in my room” she shakes her hands raising a bit higher than her shoulder, giving a dance step. Scott smiles and turns his attention to me. I know it's because of the party conversation, earlier which I had with Leili. The same thing got over my mind when Stella was giving such a reaction.

“How about playing Xbox and making Stella pissed up, making her watch us play” I wink at Scott and he laughs immediately.

“It's so rude of you” Stella pats on my hand and laughs at the same time. “I think we could go up with movie night” she answers and waits for both of our responses.

We both maintain our silence looking at each other. “So, it's movie marathon night?” I ask Stella.

“If that is so, I get to pick up the movies” Scott rushes with his voice before we could speak our ideas.

“That would not be fair. Each of us can choose at each turn” Stella tried to make a compromise. I don’t answer anything and just shrug off the thought, because I'm actually fine with anything unless I get time to spend with them.

Scott gives up “Okay fine then” and leans back to his seat in a comfortable way.

The waiter arrives with our food once our conversation is over. The remaining time we got loaded up with food in our mouth and didn't get a chance to talk over anything. In the meanwhile Stella looks up at me, like a questioning expression. It's clear on her face that she is thinking of something right now and it could be nothing apart from her father.

We didn't get any calls from him or the neighbour's house mentioning about anyone coming to the home. It is a good thing, but also keeps us in suspense like he might show up any time. I look up at my phone having a text message from my mother mentioning her status with Stella’s mom. They are having a good time as well and I'm happy about that.

We finish with our dinner and head back to home. The drive was quite pleasant and Scott was making arrangements for our movie night as we planned. Stella reaches her room to freshen up and I just watch the movements happening around me, doing nothing. She comes back in her bun hairstyle, which she does every time for her nights. Still this time it was different, wearing cartoon printed tracks and a normal tank top of her favourites. Two strides of hair are left on each side of her face and it looks perfect on her face with her smile on it. She got to the kitchen and brought some snacks with juice bottles placed on the table before us.

"Is this really necessary?" Scott asks his question with so many judgments in it. I could not control my laugh and tried to maintain not to make a sound.

Stella makes an irritated face and instead of showing it up on her brother she looks at me with her face expression. "What? Do you have anything to say about it?" She gives a worn look to both of us.

I just tried to hide my smile covering up my mouth and just nodded mentioning no. Scott clearly understood her and gave up. He slides taking his place on the sofa to my right-side, channelling into the TV with options for movies. Stella is one kind of person who could always be hungry which never lacks the amusement in me. She changes the whole mood without bothering with anything and takes up a packet of chips jumping next to me on the sofa. I stretched my arms over the sofa so she could make herself comfortable lying on my chest.

Having the remote control with Scott he doesn't decide to ask any of us about the suggestion and starts up with a movie. The movie was just a normal teenager being in college and facing some situations in his life. It was just a normal movie and it was a good one to start with. Then was the next movie of Stella's choice based upon some dance competition where the heroine is struggling with herself in making choices between her family reputation and her own willing dream. Every movie we watch was chosen in a way that none of us has ever seen before. All three of us were not in the mood to watch over the one which has been already stricken from our list of movies.

Also, each of the movies were not too long. As each of our turns came Stella leaned more closely towards me relaxing herself and Scott was completely into the scene in the movie. I looked at her thinking she wanted to say something by her shift in position and as I expected she was looking back at me.

"Why were you so silent?" She asks in a husky voice so that it would not disturb Scott. Seeing my puzzled reaction, she speaks again.

"I'm not asking now. I am mentioning the time during the drive and the restaurant." She finishes off with her lines and eagerly waits for my answer.

"It's nothing. I was just being normal." I answer her in the same husky voice in a cool manner. I then face the TV watching the movie.

She nudges me with her elbow softly to get my attention back. "I already have so many unanswered things on my mind. Make me free of it at least from the part which you can."

As usual, Stella being overthinking is not new for her to keep so many things in the small brain of hers. But still, I didn't give any response and just gave her an assuring smile. Her face becomes dull and while watching that reaction in the glow of light from the screen gives a different view of her. She doesn't question me or look at me facing the television, completely ignoring me. It annoys me of her attitude which she is good at and then I could realise how much I would have annoyed her by not telling what she wanted to hear.

"It was about the conversation I and Leili had" I confessed to her the reason for my silent behaviour for the past couple of hours. She doesn't give any surprising reaction to my reply and gives a knowing look, but still focused on the movie. "I know it would be" she responds in a relaxed way and still expects me to give a brief explanation.

I get a plan to make it come out of her mouth to confess about her conversation with Sam. The one who I don't like at all. It annoyed me that she kept it from me and I had to know it from some other person, especially not Leili. It was good that I managed with her in that situation, but still it kept irritating me for the whole time. I was the one to be angry at Stella, but the reactions she is making looks like she is being angry at me. I had a debate within myself and finally decided to give up.

"It was about Sam's party tonight" I still hold my anger and annoyed reaction, yet I manage to speak and deliver what I wanted her to realise that I was angry with her the whole time. She gives a quick reaction of shifting her position again and still not disturbing Scott with his movie. She takes my hand from the head of the sofa and holds it between her hands.

"I should have told you before her and I'm sorry, I made you angry by making you stand in such a situation with her like that. Still, you also have to know that I was not interested in going to that fool's party but since it was in the theme of my game, I had no other option and said yes. It was just to make my girls happy. They were under so much pressure for the game from the coach and other people. If I had said no then no one would have gone there." She gives a pause after her long silent speech.

I take time to go through her words and still don't come up with my own words to speak to her. Somehow somewhere still it wasn't much satisfying to me. I know I should not be like this with her, but the point is it always keeps annoying in my mind and she could have told me at any time today. I was there with her for the whole time.

She glances up once again at me expecting something in return from my expression or words and I could feel an upset on her face. "I know it was my mistake for not telling you early. To be honest we weren't alone for me to bring this upon. Scott was always around us and I don't want to talk Infront of him about this." And now she had made her point.

I decided not to put her in more trouble of thinking and turn my face towards her and give her a smile "Okay" I just didn't come up with exact words. She replies with confusion "Okay?". Seeing her I couldn't control my laugh and I hug her slightly giver her satisfactory comfort. "You made your point clear and I'm sorry as well".

Now she is fully brightened up by my confirming words. She smooches in, giving me my hug back and continues watching the movie. As many movies go on Scott yawns and checks with me asking for permission or something to have an end of our movie night and could sleep. I look towards Stella, who is already asleep in my lap peacefully. It's nice to see her in such peace. I nod to Scott mentioning we can call off our night "Can you bring a blanket for her?" I ask Scott silently.

"Else I could help you up to put her in bed" he suggests. But I didn't want to disturb her so I nodded mentioning no and he went to the room to bring what I asked for. He comes up with two blankets for each one of us and hands one to me and the other he puts over Stella. She makes a shift and gets completely comfortable. I thanked him and spread the blanket over my legs. "Call me if anything needed" he gestures his hands towards the phone next to me at the table and picks his phone going back to his room.

I lay my head back on the sofa and fell asleep eventually.

# CHAPTER 7

Stella POV:

I could feel my legs going numb and a chill breeze over my face. It feels like my whole body is rigid and has turned to stone. I could not know whether it was a dream or reality and I tried to open my eyes slowly, then I could remember I have been in the same position for more than four hours. Rob's sleepy face was facing towards me and I watched him sleep. A little of his long blonde curly hair which was kept open from his man bun style falls over her face from the breezy wind through the window which was kept open all night. His breath is so deep and it's mixing up with the sound of chilling winds. I could not move unless I could wake him up, so I managed to raise his head from my shoulder using my hands. I find a small pillow in the next sofa and I take it up to place it under his head replacing myself. It neatly fits the space by not disturbing and he goes deeper in sleep while I make myself towards the bathroom to freshen.

When I returned, he was still sleeping and I could hear my stomach crumbling out of hunger. So, I decided to make something and checked out the leftovers in the fridge. I could find only milk, so I put it to heat and tried to find the cereals to satisfy my stomach temporarily and then start to work on breakfast later eating. I was just checking through my phone and Scott entered the kitchen with yawn and his sleepy smile.

“Good morning, Stella. It's going to be a long day” he says again yawning and that is when all of the thoughts come back to my mind like a blast.

Interrupting my thoughts, I hear the doorbell ring and my heart gets a small attack. We haven't planned anything yet and I was on my nerves when the second bell rang. Scott with a sleepy head moved to open the door and a sound approached with loud noise over the house.

“Surprise” he shouted standing in the doorway, somewhat dressed up neatly and having a bag in his hand. Scott stood still watching over back and forth between me and my dad.

I know my dad has not been the same when we were as children, he has gone to training programme to overcome his alcoholic addict after divorce to take the custody of Scott even though he has not gained complete control, Scott can choose when he is 18 which is one year ahead and he is being always inspected every quarter by the government. Still the trauma he has given me never fades away even a single percent from my heart, mind and soul.

He hugs Scott in one hand “I know you guys are happy to see me” and moves him aside coming toward me. Before he could reach up to me, I hear a voice

“Hello Mr Stephenson” raised a voice from the living room disturbing my dad’s action. My dad doesn’t like Rob much which also goes vice versa and that is also one of the reasons for my nerves.

“It's glad to meet you after a long time” he steps In Front of my father standing in-between me and him extending his hand for a shake.

My dad didn't expect him here and was giving a stunned reaction “It's great to meet you young boy” he patted on his left shoulder and closed the open extended hand of Rob placing his bag down.

Rob slid him away from that place and took him to the sofa sitting together.

“Stella bring uncle something to eat, he had a long journey. Let him have something fresh” Rob made it as a sarcastic comment yet welcoming one. I give a smile watching my dad with an unreadable expression and move towards the kitchen.

Scott picks up the bag and follows me

“I’m sorry to have dad here on your day” he said in a low tone.

I know exactly what he meant, but I did not want him to worry about it even though he won't understand much of the situation.

“Everything is fine Scott and as long as you are with me by my side, I'm always more than happy as I will be” I give him a kiss on his cheek and take up the juice to the hall.

Rob keeps on talking about something which I was not able to hear until I got into that room.

“I had no idea that you were coming," he was telling my dad. “If I had known we would have changed our plan” he gave the statement which confused my dad and myself.

Looking up at me he asked “What did you guys' plan? I though you know that I'm coming even though I didn't mention exactly the time”

Rob started before I could speak something and I don't have anything in my mind to give a response “It would have skipped from Stella’s thought. Poor girl, loss of memory” he taunted me giving a wink and then turned over to my dad “We are having this outing in our college for our academic purpose which is like a one-day trip since we should start planning for career growth before we step out of college.” He then stood up and stood nearby me, taking the glass from the plate in my hand and giving it to him, continuing his speech “Since I & Stella are going out and her mom hanging out with my mom, we can't leave Scott alone in home so we got permission from our principal to accompany Scott with us which was approved" With a perfect smile and gesture of proud he held his hand over my shoulder giving me a small hug.

Scott joined “Yes it would be great to spend more time with them and that is the reason I came here, right? So, I can't miss this dad” he mentioned.

My father was giving a puzzled expression and was taking time to process all of this information over his head while drinking the juice. Then after completing it he rested the glass on the table and gave a smile “Okay so let me try talking to one of your teachers so that I could accompany you as well. Having an adult by side is not a bad idea when you focus on your career.”

Oh shit, this went out of our hands. I think we three gave this same reaction.

“It's a holiday today and you can’t ask for last minute permission. We had asked three days back and got approval on Friday” Scott continued the story created by Rob.

Thinking for a while he responded “Okay then let me find my friends in town and spend time with them. Let me know by what time you would be reaching home so that I could spend time with you guys or hope we could have dinner later then I and Scott would leave back".

Hearing this gave us relief.

"So what time are you guys leaving?" he raised a new question.

All three looked at each other at the same time. "Around 10 we have to be there on the spot" I answered to avoid clash or confusion.

Both of them agreed to me and nodded their heads in unison.

"Then you guys get ready, I will make breakfast for all of us heading out altogether".

We had no idea how long we could make it up but still felt like something is better than nothing. He was walking towards kitchen leaving us in hall and after a short walk turned towards us

"So, your mom won't be coming home today. Is she busy or she doesn't want to see me?"

"It was both of our mom's plans to hang together since we all will be out" Rob voiced up quickly.

With the agreeing nod he went into the kitchen and started doing something which was clear with the noises he was making over.

Rob bent down to Scott and whispered which was clearly audible to me as well "Does your dad really knows how to cook?" he taunts, and I hit him from behind.

"Do you really think this could work?" I asked him.

"Sure, it will. Why do you think it won't?". Yes, he was right at one point but still, him being in town makes me a bit unsure if anything might happen at any time. Rob looked at the worry in my face which is easily readable "Don't worry about anything. I and Scott will sort things out. Just go pack your things and get ready.

We have a whole day to spend together" he smiled and assured me.

"So, you have joined Scott along with your plan. But I'm surprised how easily he got along with your sudden plan" I was proud and at the same time happy to know that even Scott can match up with our wavelength and could be mature enough to handle things.

"That's brotherhood" said Scott, both waving fizz bumps to each other with their knuckles. I split up from them to my room to pack my things and get ready for the day. I pick up my jersey for the tournament match and a spare sport dress in case if needed and check all of the things in my sports bag. Later on, I changed in to my greyish black torn jean with White tank top wearing up high pony which is my usual style of dressing. After cleaning up my room and packing everything I get down when a nice aroma of food caught up my nose. Not sure what he was cooking.

I searched for both of them and they were not found, so I kept the bag in the living room and walked towards the kitchen just to make sure my dad didn't make it messier. He was standing near the stove making music from his mouth and shaking his body accordingly. He was stirring something while holding a vessel in his hand and a beep sound came from the microwave. He wore the gloves and turned to take it and then looked at me.

"I'm making pancakes and spaghetti for you kids. I'm not much of a cook, but I'm just trying my best."

Does he still remember that these are my favourites or is he randomly making which he is good at. I keep staring at him and watch his movements where his cheerfulness has been reduced after seeing me. Then I inspected the kitchen that was not messier like I thought. So, I started to take the dirtier vessels and put them in the bin.

“I will take care of it. You don’t worry. Just go take a seat and in 5 mins food will be at your service” he made a bow gesture as the servers do in the restaurant.

I was happy to be apart from him and took that opportunity, making my way to the hall.

Scott and Rob arrive at the same time, where Rob was wearing one of Scott’s hooded t shirts which has black dots in plain grey colour and it really did fit him showing up his muscles. Giving a smile to me Rob pulled up a chair and sat down next to which Scott occupied. Our dining room is a round sized and small one that can only be occupied only by four members. Dad came back taking up the plates and placed the hot food on the table which gave a stunning reaction to both. They looked at each other and Rob peeked inside to have a good look at it when the hot steam hit his face and he started coughing badly.

“I hope we can have some patience” smiled my dad and gestured to me to take a seat.

He served the red Sauce chicken spaghetti to all three of us awaiting to know our feedback and reactions to the food. I took a spoon, and it tasted good. When I looked up at them Scoot was having a casual look, Rob was closing his eyes and moving his mouth chewing it slowly in which I could say he was enjoying.

“What a lovely food to start this good day” he opened his mouth after completing his first bite.

I gave a smile “It's good to know you can cook well” I added the compliment, and my dad was giving a huge, big smile.

“I’m so happy you both like it” he grins “Let me get ready before you guys could leave” and looked at me deciding which room to choose.

“You could use the common bathroom across the hall” I mentioned, since I don’t want him to use either of our rooms. It’s a good thing we had such a thing.

He gave a sad look and, in a min, changed it to a smiling face getting inside with his bag.

“I'm still surprised with this food.” Rob said, leaning toward Scott.

He gave a smile “Sometimes miracles happen” and looked up at me.

Does he mean to say that dad has cooked this good only for me. I don’t want myself to think of it and get confused so, I pushed away these thoughts and concentrated on completing my food.

By the time we are done with food and dishes, dad came in fresh clothes with the scent of his soap. We kept a few of the food that would be enough for him.

“Okay so we are leaving, you could lock up the house and hand over the key to Rob’s mom or keep it in the regular place of their house” sending him to their house felt odd and bad for me, but I don’t want him coming with us or letting him know where we go, since I myself have no idea about Rob’s plan.

He keeps on looking at all of us. Maybe he expects someone to say something or ask him to join us. But none speaks. “Okay I'll do it” he says in a dull tone.

I move away from him, taking my bag and tug Scoot with me, both waving bye to him and Rob follows us closing the main door behind us.

As I step outside the house, I hold the bag close to my chest and keep walking in some direction.

# CHAPTER 8

Rob POV:

She keeps on walking without turning or asking anything to me or Scott. Also looking at her stern walking keeping her head down makes sure that she is worried and upset.

“Is she all-right? I hope this day goes well” Scott says in a disappointing tone and yet Stella doesn’t turn back, keeping on her walk. I went near her and tapped on her right shoulder and joined her on the left side. She turned around on her right-side seeing Scott in blank expression and then turned towards me with a questionable look.

“Lost in your thoughts?” I ask her. She gives a small nod and stops her walking, turning ninety degrees left.

Looking at both of us “So what's the plan? Rob” she gives a strong voice over my name.

“Let's go for a movie” I gave her a shrug looking at Scott for support and he understood at once.

“Yeah, it would be great” he joins.

Stella raises her left eyebrow looking at me “So this is your super plan for making my day good?”

Her voice tone was normal, but I could sense disappointment and a bit of anger rising in her. I felt bad seeing her like this and got an idea. “Let’s go skating and play games in the centre” I know this would make her happy.

She smiled and turned to Scott “Are you okay with this?” she asks him in a naughty tone.

“I’m born ready” he raises his shoulder and moves forwards hugging both of us throwing each of his arms on both of us joining in-between “I would go anywhere with you both” he adds to it.

We three turn towards my car and reach our destination. I leave them in the entrance and park my car collecting the token for charges. Stella was waiting in the counter to get tickets for us, and Scott was scanning the room checking the newly added games with its description. Our hangout place with Scott would be mostly at this place since he loves games. Once I suggested that he take up his career in this path where Stella suggested that he enter animation and coding using which he could build apps which made him completely focused on it. So, the way he looks at the games would be a completely different perspective from others.

After Stella collected the tickets, we got each one of ours and started picking our shoes to skate and then continue with other games. I sit over next to her

“So, what's bothering you?”

She was bending down wearing her shoes and her eyes looked up, maintaining the same position “Nothing” she mentioned.

“I didn't mean right now. Earlier after we left home”

She finished tying her shoes and sat comfortably leaning on the chair “I kind of feel bad and guilty” she said in a sad tone.

It wasn’t clear to me. Did I miss something? I kept staring at her awaiting for her further clear response.

“Is he really changing and am I not the one seeing it?” she turned towards me asking this question and now I understood her. “It seems like he is being the good guy doing all the good stuff and I'm looking like a villain before him. But that is not it right?” she asks and before I could answer she starts again “It's not possible. He could never change and even though he changes, the things he did which hurt us and broke our lives could never be fixed or solved.” She turns straight and puts her head down picking up her nails.

I place my hand on hers giving a comfort squeeze “Nothing can change the past but anything can happen in future.'' She suddenly turns towards me “I didn't mean to say that he is being good and you are being bad. It's just your reaction to what he has done in your life and you can't control it or you are not responsible for it.” I turn facing her and holding her more tightly than before “Just keep an open mind and be strong as you always do.” Yes, that is what needs to be done for her right now.

In a quick movement she hugs me tightly “Thank you so much.” I could hear the sentiment in her voice and hugged her back.

“Are you couples done with romancing?” Scott's voice comes up. She slowly moves from me and rubs a tear from her eyes. She kicks him with her legs after getting up from her place and runs towards the entry of skating where Scott follows chasing her. I place the bags and our things in the locker provided for us and reach towards them.

We played for the rest of the afternoon skating and dancing while enjoying the music. Stella is good at dancing but not with the skating shoes. Scott falls at times hitting and bumping other people later gains stead holding up her. They both move in a gracious way with their yellow and green shoes which are visible clearly from any place. I just follow them where at times I dash them on purpose trying to make them fall in which I don't succeed and sometimes pass through on my own way.

After that we played a few video games like shooting, car, bike racing and so on. Stella compels me to join her in the dance steps game which needs a partner, but it is not mandatory and can be played in single player mode. It is her all-time favourite game and from our childhood she has always been the top player where I always watch her winning and jumping around the place. After a few while of fun and victories we collected our points and got a small teddy which Stella held closely to her chest that she is always fond of.

We choose a normal restaurant nearby to have our food. Stella did not eat much and had a salad to have a good appetite for the match later where I and Scott ordered a large meal combo finishing up completely and quickly. I think the game we played for nearly 4 to 5 hours made us hungry. We pull up the car and reach to the ground for Stella's first big match.

"Are you ready?" I ask Stella before we leave the car.

"Always" she informs confidently and then suddenly I see her going down.

"Everything will be fine" I told her and myself.

We split up where Stella goes to the changing room then Scott and I take a place in the audience. There were only a few close members of the players being seated. The ground is being made ready by the workers setting a few things and cleaning up the floor for the game. The umpires are standing and talking with each other. Watching all the movements and people occupying the place, I focus on the entrance wishing her dad not to appear at any moment. I also thought of calling him and checking upon him to know where he would be and to have an update, but that also made me scared and don't know why. In this meantime while thinking all of these I did not notice Scott moving from the place and realised the seat next is empty. Almost the seats are filled where I finally watch him coming with two glasses of drink in his hands.

"When did you leave?" I ask him.

"I told you I was going to the bathroom" he said with a confused expression and handed me the glass. "On the way back, I found the juice counter and got one for you as well" he said sitting next to me.

The announcer started speaking over the speaker and the game was about to begin with the audience cheering up and shouting. The cheer girls with Leili as leader come forward with their steps and movements bringing up each player where the team captain always goes up with the cheerleader captain. I could always see Leili getting every chance to taunt her even though she should be the one supporting. I don't know how they still choose her to be a leader who is not doing their responsibility properly. All of the team members stand up in a line followed by the opponent team members entering the ground.

Both the captains gave handshakes while others started to stand at their position. The umpire was ready to blow the whistle and the game was about to begin. At the start the game went serious where our team was about to score but the opponent tossed the ball making sure it does not fall inside the net and our team defence was pretty good at its job making sure no one was going near the net to put the shot. Yes, the match went quite serious and after a few minutes our team had the first shot which gained the points. When it was about to go to half time, our team was leading with 5 points which is a pretty good one yet needs to be more precautious to not make them score.

The sound of the whistle came up and it was half time. All the team members came back to their coach who instructed every person. I got up and just wanted to check on Stella before she could get back to the game. She finished her talk with the members and coach and came to have a seat stretching her legs. I gave her a bottle of water that was placed in the next table

“It's going pretty well” I tried to make encouraging words.

“Still, it's not the best. Should have kept with more difference which could have been an easy win.” she said without looking at me and grabbing the bottle.

“Sure, it will be our win. I have confidence on our captain”

After completing the bottle, she turned up towards me and smiled. It was good to see her smile.

Leili came up towards us after doing her small show at half time “Looks like we have someone to watch the show” she said pointing towards the entrance.

And there it was, her dad.

My eyes bulged out seeing him and I was not sure if he was drunk or normal but definitely it is not a good thing to have him here. Making confirmation to my thought he slipped while walking and fell on the ground losing his balance.

“And it's pretty obvious he is drunk” she said in her taunting manner “Hope the captain keeps up the game” she laughs ironically and goes her way.

I turned to see Stella immediately who had a mixed emotion of tears in her eyes and angry on her face looking at him and then turning to me, with a glare.

“I will handle it” I said to her and ran to her dad.

I picked him up, raising my voice over him “What the hell are you doing here?”

He refused my hand and tried to stand up on his own “I came here to see my daughter’s game” he said in his drunken voice trying to make himself steady.

I shove him up and down “Like this.” The anger in me boils up so much. “Come let's go” I try to place his hand on my shoulders and move him outside.

He removes his hand in force from my hold “No” he shouts “I want to see my little girl. Who are you to stop me?” he shouts even louder and people around us who haven't noticed earlier watched us and started speaking within themselves.

The smell from his breath was so bad and I couldn’t bear it. The whistle goes up for the second half. If I still refuse him definitely, he will create some drama and it might disturb the game, so I decided to keep him here making sure nothing bad happens.

“Okay. You can watch the game but don’t open your mouth or make any move which might create problems that will affect the match” I warn him.

He acts like a child zipping his mouth and keeps a finger on it still dancing slightly trying to maintain a steady balance. I catch hold of his hand and turn towards the audience seat where Scott joins us.

“Are you sure this is a good idea?” he asks, helping me out.

“I’m not sure but it's too late to back out.” I say and we move towards our same place which is the third row from the game floor. We made him sit in-between us so that we could always keep an eye on him. The game has already started and I focus on Stella making sure she is fine. She seemed to be disturbed compared to the first half and the opponent team kept scoring and the game really got fired up.

At one point Stella got hold of the ball and dodged the opponent's defence in a swift manner concentrating in the game and I could see she was not disturbed at all. When she jumps up trying to shoot at the net one of the opponent players kicks her leg lifting in the air and makes Stella fall. It is definitely a foul and we could hear the whistle and at the same time the person next to me started shouting

"How dare you hurt my child?" The whole crowd looked over at us since it was silent due to the accident that happened before everyone.

He jumped up from the place losing his balance and falling over other people sitting in front of us and went to the floor shouting at that player going deep inside the ground. The coach and other people tried to stop him which was not possible and I ran toward him to stop the drama. Stella, who had fallen down sat holding her leg which seemed to get hurt, was looking directly at me and I could sense her glare.

"You have no rights to hurt her" with anger he pushed everyone who came in his way and tried to hit the opponent player raising his hand. The team members came and caught him pulling him away and pushed him down the ground far away from the place. The umpire showed the red card to the opponent player and was sent out including Stella who was hurt.

I pulled her dad away and took him out of the ground with the help of Scott and a few other members. When I was leaving the exit, I saw Stella fully focused on me when her teammates were helping her. I'm sure I have messed up and everything has gone wrong.

Once we reached out, I shouted at him "Are you happy now?" he stumbled and fell down on the road and both of us did not help him to make him stand. He was looking confused and tried to open his mouth to say something.

I yelled more at him "This is why I did not leave you inside the ground."

He looked even angrier and stood up on his feet "Who are you to stop me from my daughter. First you lied to me about the trip" he was shaking and balancing himself "And then you separated me from watching my own daughter's match" he shouted.

"This is the reason I did all of it. Now you spoiled her match and broke her again" I shouted on his face, and he stood still. I'm not sure if he had realised his mistake or not, but he did not speak anything after that.

A car with its beam light on came towards us and both of our mothers stepped out. Stella's mom gave a shocked reaction looking at her ex-husband and then looked over at me.

"I will check on Stella" she said running up towards the ground entrance.

I look at my mom "I will take these two to our home. Hope it is fine?" I asked her and she nodded in agreement. I thought it was not a good idea to take him back to Stella house and create more problems. I and Scott managed to put him inside the car and drove silently to my house.

I had put down Stella and I would never forgive myself for this neither would she.

# CHAPTER 9

Stella POV:

We had lost the game. I had lost my very first match of my final year as captain. My coach and team members were still supportive, giving much more positivity and despite being captain no matter how hard I felt inside I had to keep up a smiling face with courage to cheer them all on. I could not find the exact reason for our loss, was it our lack of practice or teamwork or my father's interruption which spoiled my whole mood. Thinking of all the things happening was going over and over in my mind creating much fuss and anger towards everything around me, but I was still at the meeting with my teammates. My mom came over and picked me up. She was just asking a few basic questions like did I have my food or do I need anything to eat or drink. I just nodded, refusing all of it and kept my silent mode on but there was a huge scream and loud voice taunting in my head and breaking me into pieces. I was not sure how to react and how to react to anyone.

When we entered home, it was dark so was my heart and mind. I moved directly to my room changing my clothes and landed in my bed. Staring at the roof I kept on thinking and thinking which made my mind hurt and my body was already so tired when I dozed off to sleep.

I felt a pain over my back and all over my body realising I have not even shifted even a bit during my sleep. The bright sunshine was hitting my face directly through the window which I left open last night. I could not hear any of the noises around me, so I tried to roll a bit and picked my phone to look at the time. It was early 6 am and I had received a few texts from Kia, Jude, Ethan, Joyce and other team members including my coach but still nothing from Rob. At least I could be happy to have such a team and friends who care for me.

The hurt in my leg started to burn and I took the ointment placed in the bathroom applying on my hurt which burned. With all the suffering both external and internal I get ready wearing a comfortable dress for another day of my life.

As I moved down to the living hall with my backpack, my mom looked at me with her weird expression, having her coffee seated comfortably in the balcony and did not speak a word ignoring my presence. Her look was as if I had made all the mistakes and nobody else was responsible for it then I realised that I have not seen either Scott or my dad since yesterday after the incident.

“Have they left?” I ask her.

She just nodded her head taking the sip and kept looking outside. Why am I getting the silent treatment? I got furious and realised maybe she is doing it on purpose to punish me for yesterday's silence during the drive back to home. I turn to my heel and head back to the front door.

“I'm leaving for college” I announced to her.

By the time I open the door I see Scott standing outside.

“Hey Stella” he says plainly. I have no idea how long he has been standing here like this.

“Aren't you late for your school?”. Is this the first thing I wanted to ask him? Yeah, maybe I've always been responsible and have prioritised him before anything else and he doesn’t deserve my anger in any way. He was helpful in more than he could have been.

“I thought I could see you before we could leave” he gestured sideways where my dad was standing putting his head down. “Also, I wanted to pick some stuff,” he said politely.

My heart whelmed and pulled Scott for a hug dropping small tears without my knowledge. He hugs back warmly.

“This is your house Scott” I say still hugging. Then we pulled apart and I let him inside standing in the doorway. I would never and ever let that person again inside my house. The anger was boiling more and more inside me to which he added the fuel asking sorry. I did not turn to his side and was standing leaning on the doorway.

What could I say to him and how could I forgive him. Even after so many years he has not changed even a bit, and this could affect Scott in many ways. I would never let this human spoil my brother's life.

“I hope you still remember that you have not received full custody on Scott.” I blurred out the words.

“Please don’t do anything like that. I swear I have changed and yesterday was a stupid mistake. I do accept it” he pleads. “I’m not like the old guy anymore. I just got angry that you guys' hid about the match and I wanted to be there to support my girl.”

“You don’t deserve to be a part of my life and you have lost it long years back. The only thing we have in common is Scott, which is not so long." Yes, I have decided to make him move away from our father once I get my job. I could never trust this guy again.

"Give me a chance to prove myself Stella" he pleads again.

I turn and stare at him. Before I could speak any more words, I heard Scott coming. So, I remained silent. He placed hands over my shoulder

"I'm sorry Stella" his voice is very low.

"You never have to be sorry for anything which you are not responsible for. I know you would not and could never hurt me or make me sad. I'm so happy to have you by my side and will never leave you. Please take care of yourself and always know I'm there for you." I say placing my hands on his cheeks with a smile on my face.

His smile brightens his face "Will see you soon Stella" he gives me another hug and takes dad with him walking towards the bus stop. I watch him passing till the corner of the streets. At that moment I wish I could have got a car and it would have been useful in many ways in which I could have also ignored Rob, where he was waiting in his car on the street.

That is when I realised, he was all the way there watching us. My body was boiling in anger and heating up. I was deciding whether to join him or take the bus and finally decided to go with him since I have an early practice and no other choice. So, I moved towards the front door and tried sitting when I got hit on my leg giving a small scream out of pain. That is when I realised, I have not bandaged my wound.

He bent forward to my knee and pulled my legs to the seat and placed my legs over him which was still painful.

"Sorry" he said and moved up my skirt to look at the wound closely. He took up the first aid kit and applied the ointment over it. I closed my eyes in pain trying not to give any sound. He looked at my expression and tried to apply it smoothly. Then he wrapped it perfectly so that it would not get infected and placed my leg slowly on the passenger seat leg rest. I felt a bit better, yet the pain was still there.

I was about to thank him and he spoke “If it gets worse let's check it with the doctor in the evening”. I didn't respond and sat watching the road straight. He pulled the car and we reached the college in complete silence. I have a reason to be angry at him and not speak anything, but he on the other side should have asked me sorry or at least give a reason or justification from his side which he did not want to and it was clear from his actions and silence. I wanted to punch him on his face while holding up his shirt and shout at him for hurting me, letting me down and not keep up his promise but everything was boiling inside of me and was waiting for the moment to burst up.

I quickly got down from the car and walked fast to the grounds so that he could not catch me, but I was fooled when he did not even try to call me or talk to me and that hurt a lot. With one of my broken legs walking awkwardly I reach the changing room and all turn to me

“Why have you come today?” Kia asked. I just gave her a shrug. “I meant you should have taken rest in this condition”. She looks up at Jude asking for support.

“Don't worry, I will be fine. Nothing could stop me from my responsibilities.” bursting these words out and thoughts of Rob who was not up to his responsibility boiled my stomach which I did not show it in my face.

Coach tapped me on my shoulder. “And that is what I call the spirit of the captain." He clasps his hand and all forms around him. “Yesterday's match was just a starting step and still we have a lot more to go. Let's not lose our hopes and keep winning in a streak reaching the qualifiers and enjoy the cup of this tournament" he ends up with a beautiful speech and all of us cheered and clapped "Get ready for practise girls" he says and calls me to his office.

With everyone getting ready I move inside with him closing the door behind. "I'm sorry for yesterday coach" I apologise.

He sits on his chair "Why are you sorry for? It's not over yet and we have a lot more to focus on. So, keep up your highs" he takes a few papers shuffled to his table.

I open my mouth to speak and he interrupts me "I know what you are going to say. What your father did was not your responsibility. As a captain you took the team very well despite everything. So always focus only on your game and keep doing the good job" he says smiling looking at me.

His words made me so happy and bloomed my dry heart.

"How's your leg now? I hope it will be ready before the next match" he says and gives me the paper with the complete details of tournament dates. "Make your coach proud."

"Definitely I will" I say in honour and move towards the ground. I was not able to do the practise but I also did not sit even for a while and was keeping up with the girls encouraging them with sprints and practises. After an hour or more my leg started to hurt and as it was going to be the end of session, I dispersed the team and moved towards a chair to sit.

I relaxed myself and jerked when I heard a voice "Should not strain yourself" he sat next to me.

Before I could get up, he held my hand and asked sorry.

"So finally, you decided to show up," I say in anger.

“I know I messed up, but I tried so much and I'm so sorry for everything that has happened”

“You messed up? No Rob, you broke me, you broke my heart. You did not keep up your promises and you let it all happen in front of you” I shouted at him as tears were breaking down from my eyes which were supposed to not come out. I should not show him that I'm weak.

“What else was I supposed to do? You saw how much effort I had put to avoid him” he raised his voice.

It made me still angrier and wiped the tears moving towards him “You could have stopped it, Rob. You could have pulled him out of the ground the moment you saw him here. You could have not let him come near to the field after he shouted In Front of everyone. You could have done more than you did and yet you did not choose to do it” I pointed my finger over his chest poking it each time I spoke.

He looked at me stunned and did not even speak a word. Good for him. I could read his reaction in his face so I turned and moved away from him, where I saw Leili watching us and I went past her in force.

# CHAPTER 10

Rob POV:

She was right. I could have done any of these things. Why did I not do it, I had no idea what I was really thinking. It broke me out knowing my complete mistake which I wasn't aware of till now. I sat on the chair holding my head in frustration when Leili came next to me and tried to console me.

"None of it is your mistake. It's all because of her dad and her fucked up family." she tried to hold me in a consoling gesture.

I pushed her hand away standing up "Don't you ever dare talk bad about her." I warned her and went to my class. I had no idea how the day passed by. The classes were boring, and I was not able to concentrate on any of them. I was not aware of the question raised to me by the teacher during the class and did not answer properly. During lunch time I did not find Stella in our regular place and had my lunch alone thinking of her. She might have gone to the canteen with her friends. I get jealous when she leaves me and hangs out with them. It has always been that I would push her to spend time with them and let me have my time for myself sometimes but this time it was weird and different the first time she had chosen them over me all by herself which hurts more than ever before.

We have not had this big fight in our life till now. We always used to have small fights or arguments in which I would easily console her, or she would voluntarily come up fighting to me. I missed being with her but at the same time I had hoped that she had not still lost complete trust in me, if she had she would have avoided me and would have not joined with me for the ride. So, this gave me a chance to console her by doing something which would make her happy since I could not change what has already happened.

After the classes are over, I go directly to the ground without taking up the route to the library because I haven't seen her after morning practise, and I wanted to see her face so badly. Also, I wanted to know how she is doing. When I entered the field, I could see her smiling and hear the voice of her laugh surrounded by Kia, Jude, Ethan and Joyce. Joyce hit her playfully and they all laughed together happily. This burned up the jealousy in me despite seeing her happy.

“Is she really that worth” I hear a voice behind me and see Leili standing next to me.

I ignored her and took a seat in the audience platform. She follows me and keeps her bag next to me, removing her t-shirt.

“What are you doing?” I shouted at her. She had put her cheer dress top inside it and I know I have overreacted.

She bent down to my ears and said softly “Nothing new that you haven't seen. Wanna look?” she bends deeper showing her cleavage which is so much visible even if you don't try to see. I move a bit away from her, taking the notes of my today’s homework. She then dresses and picks her bag, takes the shoe and sits next to me.

“So, I think you haven't been asked for prom. Would you like to be my date." She dramatically winks at me.

“I'm not interested and I’m not coming for prom. Especially with you.” I inform her sharply.

“Okay. So would you accompany me at the party after the prom?” she comes closer to me this time I flinched moving away. She then bends her head down placing her face in-between my book as her silky hair touches my hands which were holding it.

“What are you doing? Have some manners” I shout a bit loudly and take my things, placing everything inside my bag.

“You still did not answer my question” she shouts so that everyone could hear as I walk out. For sure I know Stella would have noticed all of it and will still hate me. What else could I do; I went there just to know if she is fine and was not able to be at peace because of this stupid girl.

I reach the library and set up the alarm on the phone for five mins before the time of her practice ends to make sure I don’t miss her. Even though I believe she would know where I would be and hoped would find me, yet I don’t want to take any risk because I'm not sure how she thinks now or reacts. After a few minutes of doing my homework, I got bored and looked outside the window thinking of Stella. I made her angry so I should console her and was thinking of ways to do it. She likes fantasy and is a fan of romance, true love and all those things. So, I decided to make a surprise plan in my home tonight, creating a movie set up in my room with the theme of her fantasy dream world. I called my mom and asked her plan for the evening and explain my plans to her. She agreed with me and made sure she would make everything ready at her end.

My alarm rang and I was walking to the ground where Stella was walking in the opposite direction towards me with Kia and Jude.

“Hi” I wave at all three of them

“Hey Rob, What's up” Kia joins.

“He is here to pick up his princess” Jude gives a nudge to Stella.

“Shut up” Stella says, maybe not knowing how to respond in her usual way. If she had been normal, she would have dramatically responded that I'm her prince. “Let's go Rob” she says to me, and I smile like a child watching her talking normally to me.

“See you guys” I wave, and Stella pulls me away from them. Is she jealous? Wow, I got so happy knowing it burnt her. I plan to taunt her more.

“Enough of your smile. I know what you think.”

“Is it so? Then tell me.” I jump in front of her playfully and block her way.

“Rob, it's not funny. What are you doing.” She was shocked to see my actions and was looking around checking if anyone was seeing.

“You said you know me. Then prove me”

She folds her hand and becomes her regular annoying expression “I know you planned to taunt me more knowing I got jealous. Right?” She raises her eyebrow with a confident expression.

I know she would be right still “No you are wrong.” I lied “I was thinking how I could ask for a date to Kia, or should I ask them both” I smiled. Kia likes me in a way, but it's not love. Stella would at times tell me how Kia explains my beauty and they would tease us both for fun, but Jude is a rude and weird girl who never dates a guy and has a crush on her neighbour whom I haven't seen yet probably might not see until they hang out together with us.

“I think Jude would be perfect for you” she laughs aloud and moves past me.

I follow her up "But I'm more interested in someone else." I say in her ears.

She stopped walking and her face went serious. I gave a confused look at her. She knew we were playing and how she could suddenly become serious. She stares at me for a while and then moves to our car on the passenger side waiting for me to unlock.

Resting my hand on the car, I looked at her "Hey I was just joking" I say smiling. Still her face is in the same tone. After I had unlocked, she opened and took her seat immediately. I was so confused by her change and then I came to know it might be because of Leili.

"I don't care if it is true or a joke," she said calmly.

"You know which is the truth but still I will explain. Earlier in the field Liela asked me to join her for prom and I refused it. That is why she took advantage of me which I did not like and made my way to the library" I explained with my clear words and waited for her response patiently.

She thinks for a while playing with her nails and biting it. Maybe she is replaying the scene in her head to make sure I didn't do anything wrong which could hurt her. She is correct on her side; I have lost her trust and exactly this would be her reaction after it. How can she trust my words after what I have done?

She turned to me "I know."

That's it. Only this is her response. It was a relief to me, yet I know she is not completely normal. I hope today my plan works.

"How's your leg?" I ask in a concerned voice.

"I think it's better. Afterall it was band-aid by an expert" she gives her warm smile which makes my heart bloom. I'm so happy that I could make her smile.

On our way back she plays her favourite songs and keeps singing and dancing by moving her hands and head according to the beat. It was so normal and I was happy to see her enjoying it. At times she also disturbed me during the drive and after a few minutes I joined her doing the same and enjoying the music.

I drop her in the house and reach my home quickly inside. My mom has got all of the things required for decoration. I ran to her for a hug.

“Thank you so much mom” I say and collect the things from her.

“Do you need any help, Rob?” she asks

“No thanks mom. I will let you know once I’m done and then we can start with the next step of our plan.” I hurried to my room to start my work. After an hour I complete the set up and call my mom over the stairs.

“Mom, are you ready?” I shout.

“Yes Son. I'll be on my way”. I could hear her close the front door and locked it going out.

Stella POV:

After I dressed up in my night dress and shorts, I sat up doing my homework and did not notice the time that had flown very fast. I heard the doorbell and was shocked to know that my mom was early. When I opened the door, it was still more shocking to see Rob’s mom in the doorway.

“Hi Regan. What a pleasant surprise. Come in” I say and move so that she could enter the house. “Are you here to see mom?” I ask her. She usually doesn’t visit our home much.

“I’m here for you dear” she informs in a kind way “How's your leg” she asks with concern.

“It's fine. It’s a good thing I did not have to visit a doctor for it.” I hate going to the doctor and taking medicines.

“Good.” She gave a pause and was thinking something. “I came here to ask you for help,” she said.

I nodded and waited for her to explain more about it.

“When Rob came home, we got a call from his dad and was talking about some business stuff to him, which made him angrier, and he busted out of the house. I tried calling him, but he cut my phone. I did not want to disturb you, but I have no one else to go” she said in a sad tone.

“I will call him immediately and check on him.” I went to take my phone. How he could be this hot headed to hurt his mom. I felt pity on Regan.

“No Stella. I know he will be back home once he is out of anger and reminding him that I will be alone at home.” I looked at her thinking, what other help does she need? It also made me a bit confused.

“Can you help me by giving him a surprise? I wanted to change his mood”

I smiled “Sure Regan. Anything for you. I will get ready and come back in a minute” I say and go to my room quickly. I came back in a few minutes watching her in the same position. Regan is a soft and humble person; I always admire her patience and the love she has towards her family.

“I'm Ready. We could go now. Do you have any ideas in mind?” I ask her.

"No dear and that is the reason I came up to you." She stood next to me and held my hand.

"Okay we could plan on our way. I will inform my mom and we will make the arrangements before he is back home." I text quickly and lock the door accompanying her to their house.

When we reached there, I saw his car in the garage. "Has he not taken the car with him?"

"No Stella. He just went out shouting something and throwing the vase. I cleaned up and then came to you." She was not angry at her son for such behaviour. If I had been there, then I would have scolded Rob for what he has done. Once this is over, I will teach him how to behave to his mother.

We moved to the kitchen and seeing the things she had, it felt like she was ready to make his favourite cup-cakes. I investigated the fridge, and we had blueberry so, I decided immediately

"Can we make blueberry cupcakes for him?" I said in excitement and as I thought she also got happy hearing my words.

"I think we should also make him pizza, or can we order it?" she asks. Yes, he likes it so much but not more than me. But I think we won't be having more time to cook it

"I think we can order it," I informed her, taking the vessels and starting making the batter.

She quickly goes over to the living room calling to order. I ignored it and concentrated on beating the batter with the machine and spread the sheets over the microwave plates. I know he would love it especially if he'd know I made it. His mom is so caring for him knowing exactly what he likes the most and I was happy enough that I had completed by Homeworks by the time she came. She also helped a bit by setting up the table and washing the vessels for me.

I kept the plate inside the microwave and set it to the timer then helped her out.

“I think we could also decorate his room” she informs looking at me with her beaming eyes.

I was so surprised at her reactions and smiled at her. She was making plans like it's his birthday surprise. It's so sweet of her to make so much for him.

“Okay I will go check on his room and clean it. Let me know how we can decorate it” I say to her and move through the stairs. It looked dark which made it a bit difficult to walk over. I found his door handle and opened.

My jaws were literally on the floor looking at the scene.

# CHAPTER 11

Rob POV:

She was turning the knob and struggling a bit to open the door. A little while later she entered with a shocking look on her face which glowed in the candle lights that I had set up. I made the whole room in the setup of a red and white theme where the balloons were floating all over the room with candles lit up at the corners of the room and I was hiding inside the bathroom with the door open which is next to my room door. When she stepped forward, I jumped in front of her with my red winged clothes dressed up like a vampire. She screamed out loud in fear. I closed my ears due to her horrible sound and she started beating me with her hands.

"Hey Stella, slow down" I try to stop her.

She paused and looked at my face. She started laughing loudly which filled up the room with the lights.

I know I had done a bit too much makeup since I did not know exactly how to put all that stuff. But I did my best without anyone's help and it was tough to search in my mom room.

"I will suck your blood, and I want to taste you" I tried to bring up a horror voice in which I failed so badly, and she kept on laughing more and more. She went to the bed and started laughing more falling over it. I was happy to see her laugh so much. So, I stood there admiring her beauty of happiness. After a few mins she tried to control her laugh and spoke.

"Rob, you are terrible at this" she speaks through her laugh.

I start my acting skills again "Come join me" I wave the cape behind me and try to surround it on her closing her. She hit me on my stomach playfully and I held it acting as if she had punched me hard.

"So weak vampire you are." she said smiling and stood up taking a complete look of the room and decoration. When she is done, she beams her smile looking at my face and suddenly hugs me tightly.

"Thank you so much." she says holding me tighter.

I smile holding her back "I'm sorry" I say whole heartedly. I missed this happy face of stella.

"I forgive you" she says laughing, not leaving my hold and pinches me on my hip.

I jump which broke our hug "your smell pulls me" I say in a vampire tone.

She laughs "I'm already the queen of vampire you stupid." She taunts me. Yes, we had played during our childhood like this where she would always be a vampire and I would be her victim. To make her remember it and bring happiness on her face I planned this out. I'm happy she got remind of it.

"Still, it's not over yet."

"Really" she jumps standing in her place.

Yes, this is what we do. After we played this game, we used to watch her most favourite movie, twilight's whole series for the night where I would sleep in the first half itself and once everything is over, she will just keep the tv on and lye on me sleeping.

My mom interrupts us bringing the pizza and the cakes she made for me. It was all in the plan.

"So, you also know this?" she asked my mom, and she nodded, placing the plates and the food on the floor.

"Make sure you guys don't make the floor dirty" she warns both of us and goes down patting both of us.

Stella standing in the same place hasn't moved even an inch and looked at me smiling so widely. I went toward the TV screen which was already in the movie page ready to watch. Then I sat on the floor taking the remote. She joined me keeping the food aside and we started the movie. After completing the food and watching over the first part I doze to sleep as usual.

I wake up with the jerk looking around my room filled with balloons and Stella by my side. She was sleeping peacefully holding my hands with a blanket over her. I carried her and placed her on the bed looking at the time which was early 4 o'clock and I made space for me in bed sleeping by her side.

Her phone alarm rings with a loud noise disturbing both of us and she starts to wake me up.

"This is not my usual time Stella" I say and roll over to the other side.

"Get lost" she scuffs and moves out from the bed pushing me. I went back to my sleep.

After a while I got up by my alarm and freshened up. When I came down, I saw Stella was in the dinning having food. This was not in our plan, but it was good to see her.

"Good morning sleepy head" she says without looking at me. She is talented to know my presence.

"I had no idea you guys made aware of my mom," she said.

I looked up at my mom in confusion where she smiled back at me "It was my mom's work, not mine." I said pulling up a chair next to her.

"Sorry Regan, I couldn't help you with cleaning up." Stella says to my mom. She is always sweet.

My mom brings another pair of toasted bread, placing it over my plate "You guys have classes. Concentrate on your jobs and we will take care of our works" she says with a smile on her face.

We finished our breakfast and started our way to college. The remaining days went normal and today was Stella's second match which she insisted with the coach on playing and finally got approved after showing up her skills in daily practise. I was sitting up in the regular seat of mine with other audience and the game started. The opponents were good at their game, but our team played very well and was in the lead before the half time. I was fully concentrating only on Stella and not on the game. I was so worried that she doesn't get hurt again, which might bring more problems for the rest of her matches. In the second half of the game, it got more serious and when it was about time out Stella had the ball in her hand surrounded by two defenders. She easily shifted through them and had the shot.

The whole crowd shouted in cheer, and I stood up with happiness clapping both of my hands. The whole team ran towards her and carried her away. She searched for me in the crowd and when our eyes met, she raised her hands towards me showing her thumbs up. I was so happy for her win and that she is fine. It's a good thing that the opponent team did not know her wound and used it for their strategy. A relief crossed over my face. The cheer girls came up to the field and started their performance.

After the whole game show was over, I was waiting for Stella near my car. When she stepped out of the door and saw me, she came running towards me giving a big tight hug. I lifted her up in happiness and rounded. She was screaming in joy and after a moment I landed her.

"We finally did it, Rob" she said with a smiling face and jumping.

"I hope your legs are fine." I try to stop her from jumping.

"Chill. I'm fine" she playfully hit my shoulders and moved towards her seat. "After all, I have you to look after me" she says and gets inside, closing the door behind. I smiled and took the car.

Finally, it's the weekend and I was so badly waiting for it to take a break from the classes and the main question from everyone asking about my plans after college. I hate when people keep on asking me about it. Fucking sick, man it's my life and definitely I do care about it. What pleasure does everyone find on knowing about it and trouble me with those questions ? Let a teenage guy be at peace and enjoy his life.

Just as I got ready and came down, my mom turned towards me and asked "Any plans today?"

I just muttered "No idea mom" and sat on the sofa stretching my legs.

"Your dad called," she said plainly. I know this topic will come at any time. He had been calling me every day asking about my plans after college and to take an internship in his company or his recommended company which I have no interest in at all. I have applied to a few companies in and around town. Where only two of them are big companies and the others are just a normal one. Still, I need to come up with a good plan and definitely I need to discuss it with Stella.

I just looked at my mom.

“I hope you know it's about your future and have some responsibilities on it” I walk away with anger growing up inside. I know my mom does have concern for me, but my dad doesn’t even think about me, he only thinks about his social status. He doesn’t even know what I like, what my passion is. But I can't show my anger to my mom. So, I relax myself turning to her

“I know mom and will plan for it. You don’t have to worry” I say and tap her like a pet. She likes it whenever I do that.

She gives a smile and opens her mouth to speak which she doesn’t usually do after me doing like this to her that showed how serious she is.

"Listen, your father has been more worried about you. Before he burst, I thought it would be better for me to know in advance."

I gave an exhausted look "Mom, I would definitely let you know when I'm ready."

I see Stella entering the dining room through the hallway.

"Why doesn't anyone care about Stella? She is also completing her final year with me, and she is a year older than me. So, she must be more responsible than me, right?"

She gives me a daring look.

"She will definitely make her life better. We have that confidence in her and not on you.”

"Of course, mom" she laughs, turning towards me she says softly "Isn't it getting late for the museum. I think we are already late".

Here she goes, always my lifesaver. "Yep" I turn to my mom "We both are going out and will be back for dinner. Bye mommy". I hurry up to the door before she asks anything else.

Closing the door behind us we both walk through the streets. She is making her jumping moves while walking as her ponytail hair swings in the same motion of left to right. Suddenly she turns opposite facing me and makes her jumping moves walking backward.

"So, Rob. What's about all those planning things?".

I was keeping my face straight and answered her "Please don't talk about it Stella, I'm already so much irritated about it".

She gives a cool shrug "Okay." and turns.

This is one of the things I love with her, understanding my moods. I could always count on her for my whole life.

She suddenly slips and I catch her arm to not let her fall. "Could you not watch your steps while you walk?" I shout at her. She gives a sad look and corrects herself walking straight without her wavy jumping moves. But still, she keeps kicking stones in the walkway playfully.

So rude of me, I should have not shown my anger on her when she has always been the understanding one. "I'm sorry" I kept my face straight.

"It's not a big deal. but I'm just worried that you are upset. You know you could speak anything with me". Yes, she has always been my best listener and I will be the talkative only with her.

"You do know, it's about everyone asking what plans do I have for my life after college and my dad keeps on insisting me in joining some company which he seems perfect for me"

"So, what's in that, they are your parents, and they are concerned about you. In my house also they keep asking the same question"

"What do you say to them?"

"Oh, you know me right. I just told them that I will tell them on the last day of college. Until that no worrying"

"It seems so easy for you. But it is not for me. Do you really have any plans?"

She dramatically thinks and after a few moments speaks up "I know we both can make up and come over with a plan before the last day."

"Until then?" I ask curiously.

"Keep telling the same answer which I say. And don't take it too much to your head. It's just that we must plan our steps to achieve our dreams. Simple as it is".

"Yeah, your fake dream of finding true love". She has always been obsessed over finding the true love of her life, where I am completely opposite to it.

"That's not my only dream and that is not what I was talking about. That is my lifetime achievement" she says with her eyes beaming.

"The achievement that would never happen in your life". I roll my eyes at her.

“Jokes apart. Tell me what you have decided” she asked me straight.

I looked at her serious face and did not want to tease her more, so I answered, “I have applied to a few companies.”

“Have you applied as per your dream?” she keeps her hands on hips staring at me.

God I could never escape from her. “No” I nod and put my head down.

We both have a plan of going to the same city which is preferably Seattle. Where she can start her architecture dream of working under a big company and me for now as starters work in a good company, no matter how famous they are or not and learn things gaining more knowledge on leading up a business. Even a start-up company would be the most preferable one which my dad would never allow and that is the reason I'm avoiding discussing it with them.

Later we both have decided to join and start up a new company based upon the architect and more fields whichever is upcoming and that’s all about later plans.

“How about you?” I ask.

“I have applied for an internship, but unfortunately it's not Seattle.” she mentions it sadly.

“We still have time and I'm sure we will do it.” I hug her sideways, pulling her to me.

“Just a month more.” she says in a low voice.

To change the topic “Are you prepared for the exams?”

She gets excited which I know she will be “Yes. I am fully prepared, and I know I will be the valedictorian.”

I smiled; she deserves it. She has always been good at both studies and sports.

“I think someone needs tutoring,” she laughs and starts walking ahead of me.

I hug her from behind. "So, what can we do now?” I ask her “We have the whole day to ourselves”

“We could go to the museum”

“I did not bring the camera with me” I say with empty hands. I have not even picked up my car keys.

She pulls up her bag and takes out “You left it after the match at my home.”

Yes, I remember giving it to her for checking on the pictures that were taken during the match. I don't give these to the college usually, but Stella insisted on highlighting my work so that I could get any opportunity on it. Even though I don’t work for it, she always takes care of my wishes without any acknowledgement.

We reach the museum where the antique things like cars and bikes have been placed. We aren't very big fans of it but nearby has a pond with restaurants which seemed to be like a picnic spot where a whole day can be spent. Also, despite having a car we chose the bus since we came near the stop, and it is a direct bus where we could spend more time having fun. We don’t bother with transport or anything unless we both are together. Also, tomorrow she has a match which would decide their qualifiers so it would be a good break for her today.

She keeps roaming over the museum watching each and every thing, noticing even the small features in it and knowing the details of it. I take pictures of all the things displayed and some pictures of her. It seemed like a big one where there were several rooms, and it took nearly two hours for us to complete it.

By the time we came out and was walking to the pond she was describing the architecture of the building with astonishment and awing. I was looking at the pictures deciding to make it as an album. A chill breeze hit our face in the afternoon, and I looked up to watch a clear blue water reflecting the sun rays surrounded by the green grasses with two children playing running to catch each other. I click a pic of them and turn to show it to Stella where she was mesmerised by the beauty dropping her jaw.

“Close your mouth” I shut her mouth hitting it below.

# CHAPTER 12

Stella POV:

The combination of greenery and blueish sky with water made me look at it in awe. It was a perfect place to have a peaceful mind. Rob interrupted me by closing my mouth and I turned at him.

“It's awesome” We haven't been to this place at all. I loved coming with him here today. I searched for a place to sit so that we could wet our knees by placing it in water. Then I found a perfect spot with wooden slabs near the only restaurant present here.

“Look there” I show my hand in the direction of that spot.

“I’m hungry," he says, holding his stomach.

I grin “I think we could get the food and have our place there, or else could ask them to serve there if possible” I suggest that place is not occupied by anyone else before we reach.

“What do you want? I will get there. You can go before me” he says and that seemed to be a good idea.

I ordered a soft chicken taco and some fries and he left to the shop. As I walked slowly towards our spot, I found three boys were standing in the nearby rock which was visible after a few steps and one guy among them was Sam. Oh no, I hope Rob should not see him so I was deciding whether to go back to the restaurant or go somewhere else. Just when I was about to turn, I heard a voice.

“Hey Stella '' he came towards me, and I smiled casually. “What's up. I didn't expect you to see here”.

“I just came to the museum” I threw my arm in the direction of it.

“Have you come alone? You could join us if you’d wish” he showed his boys where one was looking the same age and the other two were younger than us. “They are my cousin just visiting for the weekend” he says

“No thanks. I have company” I say, and I didnt want to mention Rob because I don’t want them to meet which might spoil his mood. Sam has always been polite and good towards me despite teasing other girls and hanging out dating each one each time. Still Rob doesn’t like him talking to me because he doesn’t trust him and always wanted to protect me from him. I also avoid Sam due to that and I'm not interested in a guy who does time pass with girls.

One of the small boys comes running up to Sam pulling his clothes to join them. “Cool. See you next time" he waves and leaves me alone to my spot grouping up with them in giggles and laughter. I placed my bag on the corner of the pole and folded my jeans till my knees so that I could dip my legs and sit in peace. I lifted my right leg and slowly dipped in the water, which was very chill in spite of the sunny afternoon. A hand behind me pushed and held me making me scared when I screamed. Making myself steady I turn around to see Rob and hit him with both my hands.

He laughed and stood next to me folding his jeans as well.

"Come let's sit" he said laughing at me and sat down which I followed.

He took up the plate of burgers, tacos and fries. We started eating and were talking as usual about the things surrounding us and nature. He also took some pictures and we were playing with each other acting like pushing into water. We spent the rest of the evening with laughter and joy. For a while it felt like there were no worries filled in our mind and I was happy for him that I could make him relaxed after the morning stress he faced.

It was about to get dark, and we decided to go home. I thought it would be better if I could mention Sam to him, else he would get angry if he comes to know by himself. So, I did not want to take the risk and mentioned the meet about him. His facial expression turned unreadable but when I mentioned that it was a small talk and he left, his smile came back and just said OKAY. I kind of felt it was not fine but still I don't want to overthink something that is not important.

We reached our home taking the bus where I slept while travelling and he woke me up once we had reached our stop. He dropped me off at my home and took off, mentioning to me to come early tomorrow. I had my dinner and went to my room tired. Tomorrow is another big and long day for me, I said to myself and went to sleep.

I felt sweaty and had a weird dream of Rob and Sam fighting over me and got up hearing a loud noise which was my alarm. I cut it out and made my way to freshen up. Packing up my bags and picking up the shoes I moved down for breakfast where Rob was already waiting for me. He picked up the toast from plates and handed it over to me.

"I hope you have brushed up your teeth" he taunted me. I was happy to see him in a good mood, but his angry face with blood staining near his lip which came in my dream taunted me more. I was staring at his lips.

"Hey. Where are you?" he says, pushing it in my mouth.

I scoffed over the food in my mouth and went to fill my empty bottle. I should never mention my dream to him and consoled myself with the dream to be as an effect of yesterday's thoughts. We walked our way to the car and the rest of the day went smoothly in practice as Rob was waiting all over in the field sitting next to Ethan and Joyce. They don't usually show up for practice sessions and it was weird to have them. Hope Rob gets along with them which usually he doesn't. I always think how he does not have friends apart from me and he doesn't talk with anyone apart from me or Scott.

After the training session we were doing our warm down exercise making ourselves ready for the match where Jude came up and sat next to me followed by Kia.

"Know what's the news" Jude draws attention from my thoughts. I look both at a time where Kia is smiling like a baby.

I looked at each other waiting for them to speak up.

"Ethan asked me for prom," Kia exclaims, and we both laugh together. "Stop it girls" she tries to hit both of us.

"I'm happy for you dear" I say and practically give her a small hug leaning towards her. "So, what about Rob then?" I tease her.

"You know he is not my type. Just because he looks good doesn't mean I would date him." she says sarcastically "Maybe Jude might suit him" she says laughing and nudging Jude.

I got stuck by her first sentence of Rob being beautiful and looked at his side. His hair was bouncy and wavy, floating in the air like waves. He kept both his hands on the next step leaning backwards seated comfortably. Is he that beautiful, I think to myself and get interrupted by Jude.

“I don’t plan to spoil Stella’s date” she says, and I turn towards her staring.

“What makes you say that? You know we won’t date” I raise my voice a bit.

“Sorry, my bad. I misspelt Liela’s name by yours.” she taunts me which makes me still angrier. It’s a good thing she is not here till now and might show up anytime.

“You know right that she asked him?” Kia asks with concern in her voice.

“The whole world knows her demonstration that day” Jude gives her statement. The words coming out from Jude annoyed me so much, so I decided to remain silent, and we all got disrupted by our coach whistle. Good thing the topic came to an end.

We reach the changing room and got ready for the match which starts in few minutes. The match went easy which we did not expect, may be the opponent team was a bit loose out of practise or my team went through more trainings and hard work. But I would always appreciate my team members either we win or lose. By the half time it was easily visible that we would win yet we still don't want to take chances. So, we played with the same energy and won the game.

The whole crowd applauded us and finally we were qualified and went into the semi-finals which is followed by next week. I look at Rob who was shouting and hugging both Ethan and Joyce in happiness. I haven't seen him this happy. We all follow our winning ritual and head back to our home. When I was out of the changing room, I saw Sam waiting a few steps ahead on the way out. Looking at me he smiles.

“Good game. Congrats Stella" he extends his hands.

I say thank you adjusting my bag to let him know that I'm not appreciating the handshake.

Ethan came running up asking where Kia was, and I answered by showing him inside the changing room.

When he was about to go inside in excitement I mentioned “You are not allowed inside".

He gave a smile and then looked at both of us in shock. I just shrugged giving an expression of not knowing anything and asking for help to save me. “Rob was searching for you” he mentions.

Good job Ethan I say to myself and turn up to Sam “Its better I hurry up” I say and wave bye to Ethan not looking up at Sam.

Once I reached the exit Rob was waiting for me in his usual place near the car. I went running up to him in happiness.

“Congrats for the Hartrick my girl” he says hugging me tightly. It made me so proud to hear the words.

I mention “Thanks to my team as well” and enter the car.

“There is no team without the captain” he finishes starting the car.

We reach my home and announce our entry to the semi-finals where both our mothers get so happy, and we all decide to have take-out to enjoy the day making it more special. Each of us orders our food and spends our time laughing and talking. But each time I could see Rob looking at his phone and keeping it down. I had no idea what was happening but felt something was wrong.

Once the food was delivered, we all had our food and Rob's mom helped us wash the dishes and we waved our bye and called for the day.

The next day was usual, and when we entered our college, the students were cheering us for yesterday 's win and the hallway was decorated with our team's name in it. Kia Jude and I joined looking at it with happy faces and were talking while walking to our class.

"Hey Stella" I heard a voice behind us, and we all turned to look at. It was Sam. "Can I have a minute?" he asks looking from me to both.

I was thinking what to answer and it was weird to have a counter with him for the past three days where each time I escaped and this time I was looking for help at Kia and Jude.

"Sure. Why don't we meet up in the class Stella" Kia says and pulls Jude to her side moving away leaving us both alone in the hallway.

I got nervous as people were walking around us watching while they passed. I smile at him not knowing what to speak.

He opens his mouth to speak and then closes backs again. Was it really him struggling so much to talk, especially to a girl. I thought to myself and opened up to speak.

"Hey Sam, What's up? Is there something you want to say?" I ask him.

"Yes" he says and again looks down, stumbling to talk. I wish we don't encounter Rob or any of his classmates and want this to get over quickly.

Then he suddenly looked at me facing directly into my eyes "Would you like to be my date for the prom" he spoke very confidently.

“What?” I spoke out loudly and that was the only thing that came out of my mouth. He was still looking at me waiting for an answer and this time I was the one stumbling with words. “Sam” I just say and don’t know what to respond. I had no idea he would be interested in going for prom with me. Then suddenly the dream I got caught up in my mind and blurred out

“No,” I replied in a strong, firm voice.

His face went sad and asked “Why?”.

I did not have a good reason to tell him. I don't even have a reason for myself I thought and said “I have plans on that day and I'm not coming for prom" I say trying to calm my voice

“Really? or have you already been asked by someone else, and you did not want to come with me?”

I gave a small laugh “Who else is going to ask me?” I say and roll my eyes.

“Okay then.” he says in a disappointing voice “If you still plan to come, let me know and I would always be waiting and ready to accompany you” he says and moves from that place leaving me standing like a statue.

Kia and Jude suddenly joined me from behind teasing. I thought these girls were gone, but they were hiding behind the pillar and listening to our conversation.

“It's not of that worth” I say and ignore them. But Kia keeps on exaggerating that I should be lucky, or does Sam really like me or just doing one of his plays. She kept on talking and nothing got into my mind as we headed to our classes.

The classes went smoothly and interesting since I had designing and drawing as two of my classes. I was left alone without any disturbance whereas in the first-class Kia kept on hinting up on what Sam asked and why I refused. I don't have any friends in this class because I prefer to be alone and undisturbed which was a relief to me. After the bell rang, I headed up to the canteen and informed Rob as well since I have not brought lunch with me today.

Usually, he is the one who would be first in our lunch meeting place but this time I was waiting for him for nearly more than ten minutes knocking at the table and exchanging my look outside and the entrance. Rob appeared suddenly and scanned the room even though he knew I would choose our regular seat. He also appeared in a different mood. I was not able to read his face so I smiled and waved at him so he could notice me. After seeing me his expression did not change neither he waved back. He just came to me quickly, taking up the seat.

"Haven't you started your lunch?" he asked.

I gave a shock reaction "I didn't bring lunch Rob. I must get some " I inform him as if it is new news for him. He did not speak anything and started taking his lunch box and placed it on the table.

I kept on looking at him.

"Don't you have to get it?" he asked, opening his box and taking a bite from it. He did not look at my face. Something is wrong for sure.

"I am. Do you need anything?" I ask and he nods in disagreement. I wait for a minute and stand up to get something for me.

When I return with the plate, I see Leili giving me a wicked smile and moving past me. I know she always used to have her lunch in the canteen but why did she smile? Maybe that is her usual thing after seeing me. I tried to avoid my overthinking and reach the table where Rob is still silent ignoring me.

After a few minutes I started up the conversation, "So how was your classes?" I ask him.

"Boring" he responds in a word and continues his work. "I hope yours would have been very nice" he says plainly, stuffing food inside his mouth.

I got a bit excited. "How did you know? Did you look at my timetable or spying on me around" I tease him.

He was in a tense mood and answered "Why should I? You can do whatever you want" and he shrugged. I knew something was wrong, but I could not ask him directly. So, I was thinking about how to build up a conversation. I wanted to ask him about last night's reason for being upset and let him know that Sam asked me for prom.

"You are my everything" I told him, smiling to brighten up his mood.

He looks at me finishing his food "Really?" he says and walks away to wash his hands and box.

Why is he asking such questions and acting strange? I was so confused and tried to stuff food into my mouth. My appetite was going bad because of this over-thinking. I put the spoon down and was waiting for him.

He came back after a while and was packing up his bag.

"Rob" I called him. He did not see me and did not respond.

I pulled his bag "Look at me" I ordered in a harsh voice. I can't take up his silence anymore.

"Leave Stella. It's late for my next class" he responds in a harsher tone.

My eyes started to get wet. I can never stand it if he raises his voice and talks to me.

“Please” my voice breaks and then he looks up at me. But still, he keeps his face in an angry mood which kind of hurts me a bit more.

I bring all my voice with confidence and ask him “Why are you angry with me? What did I do?” I ask him in a pleading voice.

He did not answer.

“I know something is wrong. Speak to me. I can't see you like this” my voice breaks even more pleading with him.

“Why should I Stella? Who am I to you?” he shouts in a louder voice and the whole crowd in the canteen looks at us.

“I don’t want to create a scene” he said and removed his bag from my hand moving away from me leaving me alone.

I broke into tears and tried to wipe it since everyone was staring at me. I stood up taking the plate and put everything in the dustbin running out of the canteen rushing to the bathroom. I nearly cried for 10 minutes without knowing any reason. He knows I can't bear his anger and yet he chooses to do this to me.

Whenever we get any fight or problems between us if he is angry, he would always inform me the reason or indicate me to be quite for a while and then later he would come with composed mind explaining me if it is my mistake or not and I would always clear it to him. But this time it was different, he yelled at me and shouted In Front of everyone without telling me any reason. I could not think of anything that I did wrong.

I wash my face and head back to class, passing the rest of the day trying to be normal. As usual I reached the ground where Kia Jude and Ethan were waiting for me discussing about something. Joyce came running behind me and joined with all of us which kind of alerted them.

“Hey Stella” Ethan welcomed me which seemed unusual.

“Are you fine Stella?” Kia asks in concern and Jude hits her with an elbow. It made me aware that they had come to know about the lunch incident.

“Let's go for practice. We need to concentrate on our next match” I said plainly, and we have a big match on the second day.

Ethan and Joyce wave at us and leave for the day. We continued our practice session where I was able to concentrate completely on the game and was in fierce mode. My workout was more than usual and normal. I also had stayed quiet for the whole session and later just waved bye to both leaving the field.

Rob was not found anywhere; I haven't seen him after lunch. He did not show up to the practice session and he was not found in the library as well. So, I went to the parking lot hoping he would be there waiting in his car which was a disappointment to me when his car was not found. I tried calling him, but he did not pick up, and it went directly into voicemail. I inform him that I'm leaving on the bus hoping he would hear it sometime.

I walk to the bus stop waiting for so long where I don’t get any since I'm not aware of the schedule. So, I decided to take a walk and to change my mind I put on headphones listening to songs throughout my journey. It's been more than thirty minutes and the cloud became slightly dark indicating rain and after a few mins it started pouring. I ignored it and did not find shelter, hugging myself tightly I continued my walk and reached home.

Surprisingly my mom was home early.

“How come you got this wet?” she asked, looking at me opening the door.

I did not answer anything and moved beside her entering inside. My relationship with my mother hasn't been so good. We don't speak much openly and as time went after her divorce and problems due to my dad still the distance between us got bigger. Mostly our communication would be just for informing each other and giving updates like reaching home late or leaving for office or college.

I directly walk to my room hearing my mom closing the door shut with the speed. She might be angry but that doesn't concern me. I did not know what else concerned me. I was not able to bear the thought that Rob has left me alone to return home and have not called till now after getting my voicemail or seeing the rain outside. I changed into pyjamas and came down to the kitchen to have something hot and was hungry due to heavy practice.

Mom was sitting on the sofa holding some book in her hand and having a cup of coffee.

"You had come early?" I ask her and open the fridge.

"Yes, due to rain they left early" she says sipping up her coffee.

To answer her previous question I said, "I did not get the bus, so I had to walk".

She did not answer anything, focusing on her current work and I continued making hot soupy noodles.

"Do you want some?" I asked her before I could start, and she nodded so I made it for both of us.

After completing my cooking, I put it in two bowls with a spoon and handed one to her, taking up the other sofa for myself with the bowl and I on the TV. I'm happy she did not bring up any conversation so I finished my food, cleaned the dishes and moved to my room.

# CHAPTER 13

Rob Pov:

She has not informed me yet and I am not sure what it is taking time for her to speak up to me. How could she do this to me? She knows I hate Sam and protect her from him which is a good thing that I do for her and us, but she has decided to go to prom with him and not even mentioned it to me. Is that prom so much more important to her than me? Where I refused Leili to be with Stella and supported her.

I was sitting in the living room staring blank at the walls and thinking all about these. My mom was talking over the phone with someone, and I did not care about it unless it was my dad. She has also not bothered to look at me and my situations where I'm suffering with my dad's trouble.

“So, what happened?” mom came to me asking this question which broke me from my thoughts and not knowing what she was speaking about.

“What?" I ask her.

“You didnt pick Stella to her home today. Why is it so?”

“I had a friend who needed help, so.” I try to sit comfortably.

She looked at me not believing “So you have got new friends” she asked.

I did not answer her and looked down at the floor. I did not know what else to do.

“She had walked all along and had also gotten wet in the rain.”

For a minute I reacted knowing she will get sick but the anger in me maintained not to show any of it “It’s her fault to not take the bus” I say

“Maybe, but it's not her fault to not know the bus timings since she was not used to it.” she sits on the sofa next to me “Maybe, should tell her to get used with it”

I got angrier and raised my voice “So she was ready to complain about it to you and not speak to me anything about what she is doing”

My voice filled the whole room, but my mom was not shaken, and she responded calmly “If you had come to know something about her did you talk to her about it first? And she did not call me and complain. I was talking to her mom, and she told me in frustration” after a while she continued “And I think she hasn’t eaten all day”

I went back to the lunch scene thinking of any image where she could have eaten. But I did not get any because I left before she could even start with her food. But I saw her getting the food. I also saw her in tears. For a moment my heart felt bad, I should have not shouted at her no matter what she had done and yes, my mother was right. I should have talked to her about it and then should have shown how much angrier I am.

I stood up and looked out at the weather to check if the rain had stopped. I took my jacket and went outside without informing my mother. After a few minutes of walking I find myself on the doorstep of Stella's house. I knocked on the door and her mom opened welcoming me inside. I ask her for Stella.

"She is in her room. Do you need anything?" she asked. I nodded and quickly went through the stairs to check on her.

I was standing near the door and was deciding what to do. I was not able to hear any sound inside and I tried to make myself calmer so that I don't hurt her again and talk clearly to her. I pushed the door and went inside where Stella gave a jerk waking up from her bed. She was holding the bunny doll that I gifted her when we were children on her first birthday after we had become friends. I know it's her most favourite and she always used to hug it whenever she is sad.

It made me quite happier to see her holding our pink bunny and it made me realize our bond and friendship. I slowly moved towards her and sat next to her.

"I'm sorry" I said and to make it clear "for leaving you in college while returning home" and for nothing else I said to myself. Hoping she would at least bring up the topic now. I was waiting for her to speak which in turn I received only silence.

When I turned to look at her, she was quietly sobbing, holding the doll tight and wiping the tears without making any noise. Stella was looking like a small child, and I dropped all my dignity and holded her which made her burst into tears.

"You have left me all alone to myself" she cried more and more.

I hugged her tightly and a drop of tear came out of me realising that I had hurted her so much. I turned her towards me making her watery crying face looking at me.

“I’m sorry. I was angry at you” I say looking at her sobbing cute little face.

“I did not do anything wrong to make you this much angry” she was pausing for each of the words and breathing heavily.

“You have to say. Without anything I would not do this to you” I try to justify my actions to her and to my heart as well.

She looked into my eyes “I’m not sure why you are angry, but before I could speak anything you were already in a bad mood and was being harsh to me during lunch”

I was thinking for a while and she had a point, I did not even let her speak.

“I know you were upset on the previous day, and I asked you in the morning during drive, but you did not even respond”

I don’t even remember her asking me, was I lost in my thoughts or maybe the music should have been louder.

She continued “I planned to ask you again on lunch and wanted to speak to you about one thing. But you were not in a good mood already and started shouting at me which made me tremble and did not have any chance to talk. I somehow planned and decided to make it clear on the evening and you were not found”

While she was speaking the tears were flowing over her eyes like a waterfall and she did not give any pause or wiped continuing her speech.

“I did not understand what I did to make you so angry that you could leave me alone. You also did not pick up my call. I did send you a voicemail” her voice kept rising like volume buttons being tuned higher. “And look now you are here” she gestures her hand at me finishing her talk.

I took the tissue box from her dressing table and using a few tissues I wiped her face. Her small make up which she had done before has all been erased and there were black lines around her eyes. It made me laugh a bit but I decided to listen to her patiently this time.

“Okay. I’m all ears. Ask me whatever you want”

She takes a deep breath “I don’t know what made you angry but just answer me this. Is it something about last night's problem that made you angry and reacted like that?”

“No,” I said.

She kept the doll in her lap and holded my hands “Fine, we will come to that later. I was thinking this whole while and had an intuition that you might get angry on what I'm about to say to you and that is somehow linked to all of this”

Here comes the problem. I try not to express anything and remain in the same position.

“Please don’t get angry and hear me out completely” she says, and I nodded my head agreeing with her.

“Today before we went to our class Sam came to me and asked me to join him for Prom, but I refused”

This shocked me. “What?” I asked her. “You said no to him”

She was scanning me for a moment with a confused reaction “Yeah. I know you don’t like him and how would I say yes to him. Listen I know I'm more than excited for prom but that is to go with you and not with anyone else” Her words were clear.

“But” I stopped before speaking and took my hand from her, turning the other side. I was so confused.

“But what Rob?” She came closer to me.

“I heard you said yes to Sam and the whole lot was speaking like you both were going to be prom couples” I stammered “Also” and I was struggling for words and looked at her face.

She was confused as well.

“What did you hear, Rob?” she kept asking.

I did not want to say the bad things that I heard about her and make her even more upset. I have made a fool of myself by letting their words go through my thoughts infecting our bond.

“So was this the reason you were angry at me thinking that I have told yes, and you believed them instead of confronting it to me” from her tone it was clear that she is pissed off.

“You believed whatever they said and did not trust me. You left me all alone believing the gossip that ran around you” her voice was breaking, and she stood up in anger or broken which I was not sure of.

“Leili made it so sure of it” I say suddenly and then close my mouth realising the mistake.

“Oh wow." She clasped her hands “So now you believe her and not me.” she shouted in my face. We stood faced with each other. “Where do I stand Rob?” she shouted in anger even though her eyes were wet with tears. She was on the edge of bursting out.

I just then realised how big a mistake I have made, and I need to calm her down before she hurts herself again. I have been so stupid, and my judgement has clouded my common sense.

“I need to know what you heard and believed. I think both are the same” she said in a disappointing tone.

I gathered all my courage before I could speak to her. She deserves the truth.

"When I was about to join you for lunch, I heard Liela's friends gossiping and mentioning your name. Initially I tried to avoid it, but I couldn't when I heard Sam's name. Also, I was filling up my bottle and heard them telling bad of your character and you might have dated Sam cheating on me or flirting with both of us" I try to bring up words because I can't tell exactly what they spoke since it was too bad, and it would hurt Stella. "Then Leili came up looking at me and kind of insulted me for being your friend and you don't deserve me kind of thing." and I was stammering.

Stella was looking at me astounded "So you believed all of it" she asked me.

I immediately made her sure "No. I was only angry that you had said okay to go to prom with him and because of that it gave space for them to talk about all of this rubbish stuffs" I responded in anger.

She did not respond and was still going through my words turning the other side keeping her mouth wide open and placing her hand on it in shock.

"So, you did not decide to confront me for the misunderstanding you had and instead left me to suffer."

Yep, exactly that is what had happened, and I feel ashamed for admitting it to her.

But I also wanted to give her clarity on the evening incident. "But in the evening, I did not leave you on purpose. I was waiting in the library for you and a guy fainted. The only person with a vehicle in the library was me. So, in an instant I went and helped taking him to the hospital. Also, when you called up, I was in hospital with him handing over the details to his parents and came back home"

Still facing the other side, she said “But still you did not get the idea of how I would come back home. Also, you did not call me back after seeing my missed call or voice mail”

How is she asking such valid questions which is making me more guilty of my stupidity.

She turned and stared at me waiting for my answer and now it was her turn to be angry at me.

“In that case, I did see your call but did not hear the voicemail. Also, in anger I kind of felt like you would come home with any of your friends or with him”

She was just nodding talking silently “if I have more friends, it doesn’t mean I will choose them over you" and then her voice raised “Where you always tell that I'm your only friend and I'm so important to you and yet you judged me by yourself and your girlfriend’s words leaving me all alone left in the road to suffer”

She sat on the bed “Great” and took a deep breath.

“She is not my girlfriend” I said in a sharp tone. I hate to think of her like that.

Stella just stared at me in anger, and I know I’m not in a good position to justify myself when the whole mistake has been on my side. She was about to tell me, and I had overreacted just by listening to those girls' words. How did I make them enter in-between me and Stella so easily?

I can't compromise Stella easily on this, where the only way to console her was done at my last time apologising effort and this time it must be more than that which I have no idea of.

I kneeled before her lying on her lap and holding her around her hips asking sorry and it was genuine. I did not know anything else to do other than accept my mistake and plead to her.

# CHAPTER 14

Stella POV:

He had hurt me but now he realises his mistake and is begging for my apology. I can't bear to see him like this no matter how much I have suffered. I place my hand on his soft hairs and remove the band which he always uses to keep it tied. After our high school he wanted to do a change over on his looks, so I suggested he grow more hair and tie it up behind. Initially he was finding it a bit harder to make it grow, but in three months of time he successfully achieved it and till now he is maintaining the same style.

I ruffled his hair and I loved playing with it, which he usually would not let me do. This time he just looked up at me smiling and shook his head where his wavy hairs were still ruffling.

“Thank you. For everything.” he said and lay down again on my lap letting me play with his hair.

I will always be there for him no matter what happens. I promise myself and we spent a few minutes resting in the same position.

Waking up on the next day I was smiling thinking of the previous rider coast day and yet finally I had happiness in me. Also, there was pressure of the match which ends by this week followed by exams for next week. I scoff and lay down in my bed for a while trying to absorb some energy for myself.

Finally, I got ready and moved to college for morning practice with Rob where we were discussing the exams, and he was enquiring about my match preparations. That time it struck me.

"You did not tell me your reason for being upset on Sunday night" I ask him

"It's nothing," he said, looking straight down the road.

I hold his hand on the steering "I don't want to pressure you asking about it, but know one thing that I'm always there for you"

After a few minutes of thinking he answers, "My dad would be home next weekend."

"It's a good thing Rob. You could spend time together and be happy that it's after the exams. You could also skip prom using this excuse"

"It's not that simple Stella. He says that he has something to share with mom and I don't know what it is. Also, mom is not the same after that. She is hiding something from me" he says in a tense mood.

"Do you think it has something to do with your career?" I questioned him and he nodded.

"I'm not sure. Every time he comes home, he always creates some problem disturbing my mind and peace."

Both of our fathers are similar in this way. I smile thinking of it and Rob looks annoyed.

"Listen, don't put all these in your mind. It may disturb your exams. Whatever it is let's face it later and now let's focus on the present"

Agreeing to me he says "You are right in one way. Did you talk to Scott? Is he coming for the finals?"

"Yes, I think, and he promised that dad won't be coming for any of it. Both for the final match and for graduation." I then smiled at him "You are pretty sure that we would be into the finals"

"You deserve it Stella and I know you would" he holds my hand in a comfortable way.

"Same Scott words" I smile at him, and we reach college.

The practice today was hard, and I was draining everyone's energy, instructing them sharply to focus on the game which is on the next day. I decided to make them relax by tomorrow and that was the reason for today's hard practice. Coach came by to look at my training.

"I hope your strategy works." he stood next to me "We will discuss the plan in the evening with the team."

I nodded and moved to the field with my team to work out.

Kia and Jude were so much sweat coming to me both said in unison "Too bad Stella"

I giggled at them "Nothing is easier my friends" I say and change my shoes.

They both hit me playfully and we changed to our regular clothes taking up our classes for the day. The evening went as planned with less workout sessions and planning for the match. My speech made everyone in fire burning inside to win the trophy.

By evening when we reached home Rob wanted to go quickly to prepare for his exams and yet we had our gossip talks where he also informed me that he has completely ignored Leili despite she tried to talk to him twice today and I joked to him that I did not see Sam at all it's like he has disappeared which Rob also agreed and we left to our homes.

After my house work and completing all my college stuff, I call Scott.

“Hey buddy. How are you? What's happening?” I hear some loud noise behind me.

“Hey Stella, I just came out with a few friends to play. We are also planning to build up a new game. I will show you our plan this weekend.” he says excited “And all the best for tomorrow's match. I want you to see in the finals holding the cup.” his words were beaming.

“Hoping we will make it happen. Let's see” I say, and I was wanting to ask him about dad. How he is doing after the previous weekend of his activities. I don’t want Scott to be suffering due to his drinking habits.

“Stella, I'm in a hurry right now. Will see you on the weekend and we can talk loads. Take care and update me tomorrow.” he says and cuts the phone with bye.

Once my mom was back home, I finished my dinner with her and went to sleep.

Morning during breakfast mom started

“So today is your semi-finals, right?” she asked, and I nodded putting the bread into my mouth. It was late, and Rob was already waiting for me outside.

“I’m sorry I could not come today” she says and while I was about to move out through the door, she held my elbow stopping me. I turned to her and looked in shock “Hope you will let me watch the finals” she said smiling.

It was great to hear those words from her “Sure mom” . I turn and hug her, feeling the warmth.

When I reached the car to take my seat Rob gave his wicked smile “What a mother daughter love” he teased me.

I hit him and informed him about my mother's surprise act where he was happy to hear it and we left for college.

We did not have our morning practice, yet we all met up in the coach office and had a few discussions of the match timing and preparations before that. Also, the venue for the match had been changed to our college which was surprising and made an urge to win this match. It’s a home game for us which can never be lost at any point, and it is going to be tough.

During our way to class this was the discussion between the three of us and at my lunch time I was speaking more of it to Rob. Maybe it has been the talk for the whole college where the preparation started during the second half of the day making me still nervous, but I have confidence in myself and my team. I can't let my loved ones lose hope in me. All of them were eager to watch my finals and win the cup.

At the end of the day all the pressure was upon me, and I went with my team to the field. The whole audience was shouting, holding up the cardboards and cheering loudly when we entered. My eyes scanned the crowd and searched for Rob who was sitting in the same place smiling at me. The cheer group did their performance and the announcer spoke over the mic which I did not listen to.

He called up the captains for the toss and we had lost, so the opponents chose the side according to them. I always don't believe in this superstition and believe in hard work and practise. Our team gathered around me, and we went into the field taking up our positions. The sound around me became lesser and my breathing was heavy.

Hearing upon the whistle sound I took the ball and moved towards their side passing it to Jude. She caught up my thoughts and went according to our plan and placed the ball inside the ring. It was an instant and quick move by us where we placed within the first ten minutes. It was a huge move, and everyone cheered up when the rest of the team joined us. As the match went in the first half there were few fouls at our end which gave them chances to score the goal and by half time, we were lagging 10 points from them.

I rounded up the team and instructed them not to take up the pressure and play it with a clear mind and happily like our practice session where we always focus only on our game forgetting our outside world. Rob came down running up to me, but I ignored him and moved with my team. I hope he understands that I can't let myself distract and my team needs me more.

Second half started and the ball got slipped again from us twice and they scored leading with 20 points. I Kia and Jude came down and talked planning our tactic move forming in threes and moving around the opponent players not letting them know our actions. This made easier to confuse them and we placed the score. It was win for us and we continued the same strategy but this time with other three members where the opponents got easily confused and distracted.

The sound from the audience went mute for me and my whole focus was only on the game. I didn't even look up at the scoreboard. I just wanted to do the best without thinking of the result. The same strategy was done by each of the three members which we had already decided in the morning and shuffled as per our plan to confuse the other players scoring easily. But at one point one of them found and while Kia was about to score, she pushed her making to fall and it was a foul.

The referee came and showed only warning to the opponent girl and she gave wicked smile to us. Later, she was always focused only on three of us which made a little difficult for us to work our plan, but even though we did not let the opponent to score as well with our strong defence players. I was so involved into the game and got disturbed when I heard the whistle sound mentioning the time has been over. Before I could even realise the scores, I heard the announcement making that we have won the match and have moved to finals.

All my team members came running up to me including the coach and they carried me. I was laughing out of joy and my whole teeth was visible. It was an awesome match and evening to celebrate. Coach then gathered us after the celebration informing us that we have the finals on Saturday and we all cheered up. He also reminded us to keep up our grades for the exam which is as important as our games. Before we could disperse Leili and her other cheerleader friends were standing outside the changing room and congratulated making noises. I know she is creating some kind of scene to draw all of the attention towards her.

“Kudos to all my lovely ladies” she said “I would like to have a winning party for all of you at my guest house” She started clapping around.

“We still have the final match” I say out loud

“Don't be a party spoiler.” She tried to insult me and turned to others thinking they would support her.

But my team members do respect me, so they all said in chorus "We agree with our captain."

"We need to focus on our game right now" said Jude from the crowd and everyone nodded in agreement with her.

Leili scuffed but then regained her voice telling us "Okay great, then we could have it after our final match. I know you guys would win" she shouts raising her left hand above and everyone cheers getting dispersed after accepting her invitation and agreeing to the party.

"She doesn't even miss a chance to show up her money" Kia scowls.

I giggle and move away from that place. I don't wish to be in that toxic place anymore.

I run to Rob who always waits for me. He hugs me tighter than ever and speaks slowly in my ears.

"I have another piece of news for you".

I move my head back and look at him questioning "What is it?"

"I have got into an internship programme of a start-up company" he beams with a smiling face.

I jump from my place in happiness and ask more details of it.

"Guess the place" he taunts my curiosity where I was not able to think, and he said "Its Seattle" and he carried me in happiness.

I laughed out loud, and my world was spinning. I was happy for him, but a disappointment hit me that we must stay away from each other after college for a job. I could not think of a life being away from a person who has been from my walking stage.

“Great” I congratulate him for not showing my sadness and ask him “But we are not done with our exams and results. Then how come?”

He shrugs “Even I thought of it. But they have mentioned in mail clearly that until my results come, I would be an intern with a stipend and after that based upon their requirements, they would make me their employee if I have good results.”

It was great news, and I was happy for him wholeheartedly with a pinch of pain which I had to work it out alone by myself.

“I have decided not to let them know before the exam gets over” he says to me and tells me not to tell it to anyone and I promise him, thinking maybe I could use this period of time to console myself.

# CHAPTER 15

Rob POV:

Stella is always my secret keeper and supports me no matter what. I'm happy for the news I got but I could see her face going a bit sad on hearing it but also, I could know she was happier than me. We reach our homes and inform only about the match and my mother hugs Stella in happiness. I could see Stella's mother being happy as well, but she doesn't express it as much as my mom did. She just gave her a proud tap on the shoulder with a smile on her face. Also, on the exact time we got a call from Scott and was speaking for hours where I and Scott joined together taunting her.

Despite all these happy things happening around us I was worried about how to convey the news to my dad and about his arrival. The worry about my exam was nil since I was completely prepared and I'm not the guy who reads at the last minute whereas Stella is opposite to me, but I couldn't be such a great multitasker like her. She manages her family, sports, extra-curricular activities and studies as well. We finish our dinner soon and wave goodnight to everyone reaching my home.

On Friday evening I was waiting for Stella in the field where she had finished her practise and came from the dressing room running to me.

“Scott would be coming tomorrow” she beams in excitement.

“I know. He had already pinged me and I'll pick him up tonight”

She looks at me with a wicked smile. “He did not tell me that he would arrive today"

Oops I've broken the surprise; I thought and bit my tongue.

“Sorry, surprise spoiled. Don’t let him know about it and act surprisingly” I say in nervousness. If Scott comes to know that I have spoiled it, he will beat me.

She laughs “Okay” and continues “Anyhow I am happier for his arrival so it would be a surprise reaction at my end” she winks “You don’t have to worry about it.”

I admire the love that Stella has for her brother. Sometimes I used to think that I could have had a sibling of my own, but Scott had never made me feel for that. He has always treated me equally with Stella and would say that we both are his favourite person in the world more than his parents or anyone else. It makes both of us proud and responsible as well.

We plan for this weekend on our way back and she informs me about Leili’s party.

“Did she invite you?” she asks

“I haven't seen her this week.” She looks at me with a questioning reaction on her face. “It’s true. Except on the field during your match I have not seen her.”

She keeps her face one side smiling, bending looking more at me.

“I don’t wish her to see after what she did to us” I stare at her, proving to myself that I'm telling the truth.

“I don't think we can completely blame her for it.” She taunts me, which is fun for her but it's kind of irritating for me to bring back all those bad things that happened and reminding me of my mistake. Stella always does this taunting me until I completely accept and until I get relaxed whenever those topics pops up. Even though I got pissed up at that moment, this action of hers has been very useful for my self-development which I could realise after a few days.

I take a deep breath which she notices and talk quietly. “I know what you are doing, but until I get myself steady, I feel it is good to avoid her” I spoke the truth.

She nods and to change the topic I ask her back.

“So, you are going for the party”

“Never” she responds immediately “Do you want me to go? Or do you want to join with me if I go”

I hit her with my elbow, and she acts as if she has been hurt by mimicking the noise and we both laugh out loud.

“I also heard another news” I again changed the topic.

She asks what and then beams “I’m sorry I forgot”

“How could you forget this big one”

She shrugs “May be due to Scott’s surprise”

Yeah, she is right and has a point. “Okay accepted but I wanted to hear from you”

She blushes “I’m going to give a speech on graduation” and she covers her face by hand.

“Be proud to be a valedictorian. It doesn’t happen to everyone, and you are a special person even to college. I'm bit jealous, but still happy for you”

“Did you wish to get it?” she asks in shock.

“No”

“Then why are you jealous?” she looks confused.

I laugh “I’m because you are one and only my special person but now you have become to college too”.

“Even for Scott,” she says, hitting me.

“For Scott it's not only you, it's we both” I stick my tongue out taunting her

She says dramatically “I’m still surprised how everyone chose me. I don’t have the highest grades”

“Maybe they choose you for your multi talents.” That might be true.

She goes silent agreeing to my point.

We reached my home, and she spent some time with my mother while I was packing a few things for the weekend to stay with them, which is usual whenever Scott arrives, and Stella’s mom will sometimes stay with us only if my mother accompanies, else both of our mothers would stay in my home. Their family has always been weird where Stella and Scott don’t have much bond with their parents and vice versa.

When I reached downstairs hearing, them talking loudly and giggling, they became silent after seeing me.

“What's going on?” I ask suspiciously.

Stella answers “Nothing” and shows me to start talking. She was mentioning to inform my mom about the internship which I was not ready still. I preferred to inform only after our exams and that would be better. My mom saw our non-verbal communication.

“What's going on between you two?” she asks, hitting playfully over Stella.

“Nothing” this time I answered quickly before she could begin something and put me in a trap.

“Don't plan anything mischievous kids. There would be severe punishment if you get caught”

I jump up next to her on the sofa bouncing “Only if we get caught” and I wink at her.

She hits my head playfully.

“And by the way thanks for giving the idea” I say and get up immediately before she could hit me again and reach the doorway.

Stella reached me “Don't worry mom. I will take care.” she assures my mom.

We laugh our way out when my mom waves bye and I drop Stella in her home. I reached the bus stop after a few minutes to pick him up where he was already waiting. I opened the door for him when he approached.

“I hope I did not make you wait.”

He nodded in disagreement while taking up the seat and was exclaiming and speaking in excitement to watch his sister in surprise.

“I also have another thing to tell you” Scott speaks in a serious tone suddenly.

I look at him in an expression of asking what it is about.

“My dad might come tomorrow to the finals.”

It shocked me and I put up the brake, thank God we did not have any vehicle behind which could have hit upon us.

“I’m sorry, he heard me while I was speaking to you about the plan for surprise and don’t get angry with me” he stammered getting scared.

I still give a shocking reaction to him not knowing what to say and how to reply. I can't make Stella upset again knowing that I failed last time and now it would be more difficult than that.

“Don't worry he promised me that he would not drink. He also said he wanted to be there for her, and I was not able to argue to that point” he spoke helplessly.

“Unless and until he doesn’t create any problem it’s a good thing” I think to myself that it would be great if her family gets united in a good way and gets happier. What else more do I wish for than watching her happy. I don’t remember the last time when they had been together being normal without any problem. Maybe I should inform my mom and take her mom as well to watch the final and support her.

“Is it a good thought to keep it from Stella?” he asks.

“It is. If we inform her now, she would be worried, let her know before the match watching him steady and we both are there to manage right. Let's not make it go wrong this time”

We reached home and Stella opened the door before we could get down. Watching Scott, she came up running to him and hugged him tightly in happiness. I park the car properly and take his luggage holding it in my hand.

“I’m so happy to see you” she beams with happiness.

He put his arm on his shoulder "I wanted to spend more time with you guys" and he pulled me on his other side placing his other arm over my shoulder.

We three walked through the door and I could smell something delicious, and I looked at her.

"What has mom cooked up for me?" Scott asks, turning to her.

She smiled mischievously.

"Don't tell me it's you" he gets surprised.

I explain to him that his mother has already reached my home and only we three of us are going to spend the rest of the weekend here.

He gets happy and looks again at Stella waiting for the answer for his question about food.

"I tried making it and hope it will be nice" she spoke shyly, and it was different to see her like this. She is not the best at cooking and at times she would only help either of our moms. Even when the situations came where she had to cook, my mother would not let her and always be there for us.

"I'm waiting to taste it," he said, landing on the sofa "I have planned to be here until next weekend."

"You are staying for graduation?" We both asked at the same time and looked at each other.

He gives a big laugh nodding his head "I love you guys" pulling both of us to him hugging and we fall on each other in that small sofa.

Stella, stuck in-between both of us tries to say "It's going to be difficult for my exams" and she makes a frown face.

“I think we all can be together in either of our houses” I give my suggestion and I could know both are happy with that.

“That could work” she says and pushes me on the other side moving to the kitchen. “Go freshen up boys, let's have our dinner”

Rubbing his stomach dramatically, he says, "I'm very hungry” and gets up.

I follow him mentioning “Hope it's good" and wink at her.

After a while we gathered in the dining place and Stella had arranged all the dishes in a perfect manner which was colourful tacos filled with vegetables and cheese followed by brown roasted grilled steaks supported with French fries around it decorated with a glass of drink for each one of us. It almost looked like a perfect dinner as in a restaurant.

Scott came behind me with his expression “Wow. I could not believe you had made all these” and I agree with him on this.

I look at Stella where she has her curious face waiting for us to taste and give her the feedback. We both compelled her to sit with us so that we could have it together and enjoy ourselves.

The moment I tasted the steaks it was melting through my mouth and went inside quickly. It was perfectly cooked and was easy to cut. The taco was crunchy and tasty with the tango sauce she had filled with it making everything taste in equal proportion.

“I don’t think I have had such a yummy crunchy taco in my life” I applaud her for the efforts she has done and still surprised to know that she would cook this well.

“Everything is so perfect Stella” Scott joins me.

Looking at both of us Stella’s smile was so big, and she also started eating. There was also plenty of food for all three of us and I could say we all had stomachs full not knowing how It went inside. I acted like burping and rubbing my tummy as we laughed together loudly.

After finishing everything and looking at the empty vessel and plates we laughed teasing. I helped her clean the dishes whereas Scott was arranging the bed in the hall for us to sleep.

This time we did not want to watch a movie and instead chose to play. We took a monopoly board which has not been touched for more than six months and played till midnight. Then we packed the game having a few gossips teasing each other and slept with happy giggles.

# CHAPTER 16

Stella POV:

This day is going to be another big day in my final days of college. I want to make myself a proud captain and an honourable student. Giving a speech on graduation makes me nervous but more than that I must concentrate on today's final match. Rolling over I find both of my loved ones sleeping next me snoring and putting their legs and hands upon one another. Being with them I could achieve anything and need not worry about any such negative vibes. I try to get up without disturbing them by pulling my dress which is stuck under Scott.

After freshening up I plan to make waffles and pancake which is a regular breakfast for our weekends. I get a few texts from my friends and teammates based upon the plan and reply to them acknowledging to meet up in ground by afternoon three o clock.

Suddenly a voice distracted me

"The delicious smell woke me up" he says, holding me behind my ears softly.

I smile and concentrate on beating up the batter.

“I did not know you would be a good cook”

“Me neither” I laugh a bit louder, and he shushes me.

“Don't wake Scott up. So, what's the plan today?”. I could hear his breath while he was whispering in my ears.

“We have planned to be on the ground by afternoon until then I'm going to spend my happy times with you”.

“I want to tell you one thing” he says which makes me nervous hoping not to spoil the good mood we have.

“What?” I ask in a dull tone.

“I have some errands by afternoon,” he said. I kept the vessel on the slab and turned to look at his eyes. There is something he is not telling me, and I can know it for sure.

“Are you fine?” I ask him worried.

He smiles and pulls me closer. “It's just I need to check on mom and clean my room with a few things and things. Also, I would bring both of our moms to match so I must go right.”

He tries to make a point, but I still could not get satisfied with it. I put my face down thinking how to pull words from his mouth.

He takes my chin up facing him again and looks into my eyes with his beaming golden eyes.

“Don't worry, everything is fine.” he says and pricks my nose.

“If anything, you should let me know. Don’t keep me in the dark.”

I hope everything will be fine, I assure myself.

“Don't make me suffer in hunger” he says dramatically, placing his hand on stomach and keeping a pity face.

“Go brush first” I push him aside and he goes to the room.

Even if he is not fine, I will always be there by his side. After a few moments Scott awakes, and I push him to freshen up when he comes running to the kitchen and to taste the batter before I could cook. We all then arrive at the dinning and have our breakfast. Both complimented me for the good food which made me proud and happy. Maybe my cooking skills are developing.

The rest of the afternoon went just like that where Scott was explaining about his school life and about his new project that he is doing with his friends. It made me feel good that he has some good friends over there. At times I think of joining him into a hostel and decide that for college he must move out of town and will put him in a hostel at that time. I can't let the troubles disturb his career and growth. By next year I will earn and will get a good amount in hand which would be easy to execute my plan.

Each of us gets ready to move out and cleans up the house, splitting up each with a task. We completed it soon even though we played a bit and made it even messier. On time we got ready and started to leave. Rob decided to leave Scott with me on the ground when he went back to his house and yet he hasn't given a valid response even when Scott was insisting on being with us.

I met up with the gang and spent a few of our giggles to make our mind relaxed a bit and when the coach came, he started with the same vibe. Later the topic and discussion went into serious planning up for the strategy to be played in the match.

We all decided our positions and doubts were cleared everyone dispersed to get ready. I was picking things from my bag slowly thinking of Rob. He hasn't texted me anything and I was not sure that he has reached the ground or not. I was debating with myself whether to either call him or not. I was worried thinking about him and saw Kia calling upon me with Jude by her side showing me outside to join with her.

I find Ethan and Joyce standing having some flowers in hands and looking at us they give each one a flower. I got white Daisy and a pink rose where they both got different colours but the same flowers. Looking at the flowers it made me smile

“What's this for?” I ask them both.

Kia nudges me “Don't be rude Stella. It’s a gesture of wishing luck” she looked at Ethan with her wide smile.

I nod “I’m not rude” and I look at both “Thank you so much guys. This means a lot”

They give smiles and nod wishing us luck and kia hugs Ethan which kind of seemed weird to see my friends dating.

When they were about to leave, I call Joyce

“Did you happen to see Rob?” I enquire him to know the update.

He shrugs and Ethan answers, “I think only your brother was up there.” and after a pause he added “We could check and update if you wish”

I give them a fake smile “I don’t think it's needed. Thanks anyway” I say to them and wave going inside. Good thing Kia and Jude did not notice it.

We all were ready to enter the field waiting for our call and jogged in line when the whole crowd was cheering up. With all those lights and crowd once I reached a place to stand, I looked at Rob’s regular place where I found only Scott sitting waving at me and shouting. I scanned the whole crowd but did not find him.

We then split up to our side waiting for the match to start and I saw both of our moms coming and not him. After a few minutes I see my dad’s appearance in shock and turn around to see Scott where he had already started to run towards me. By the time he reached near me he started speaking.

“Don’t worry. He is just here to watch the match and I will make sure he does not create any problem.”

I was shocked. “So you know it?” I asked him.

He nodded his head in approval and before he could leave to dad, I pulled him.

“Where is Rob?” my voice was more demanding which I did not realise until his response.

“I don’t know” he looked disappointed by my tone.

I left hold of his hand and let him go. Everything going on around me, and his presence not being here worried me a lot but once I heard the whistle sound and the look on my coach's face, I made myself focus on the game and not to think about anything else.

The match has started, and the strategy was going well with few disruptions. Jude has started with scoring followed by the opponent with few scores leading to us and they started blocking her. We changed the game plan on the spot and scored a few more goals trying to cope with our opponent and unfortunately by half time we were lagging twenty points.

Whole team gathered around me with exhausting breaths. Everyone was tired including me. The opponents were so tall and were very quick compared to us. It was tough for us to score but I was proud that we still managed to get points. I boosted up our team's confidence and told them to concentrate more and keep continuing the good play.

My mind was wavering to check on Rob, but I did not have the guts to do anything which might affect the match. So, I did not turn to the audience and entered the field. I was able to hear the crowd cheering and roaring consoling myself hoping he would be one among them.

The game went more serious where we had few fouls as well as the opponent team and yet they managed to keep scoring where it got tougher for us to follow them and did not have a chance to lead them in scoring. The running made everyone tired. My teammates and myself played so hard to catch up with the opponent scores, not letting them go forward in the lead. So, by the time it was about to end we scored at the last minute and made the scores tied up.

Even though we had not won for now, taking up for overtime was a success to us. When the overtime was added and was acknowledged, I immediately sprinted up quickly which made the opponent get confused and placed the score. After that we made a good defence and did not let the opponent get near the ring. Even if they had reached, we made sure for them to find it difficult to place the ball inside the ring. Good thing we had one tall person in defence, she did her job so well which avoided our opponent to score. And after that Jude collected the ball going through gaps and came running to the opponent side where Kia and I were waiting.

We had our kind of thing which no one would understand and executed it, placing our score and the time went out. The announcement came for our win and we three ran towards each other and hugged tightly. Our other team members surrounded us, and it was a wonderful moment of our life this year.

In the happiest feeling I turned around to look for Rob pushing the crowd a bit wide to make my view clear and I did not find him which brought so much disappointment in me, also I got more worried not knowing where and how he is. He would never miss my match, especially today. What is the reason that has stopped him? Many thoughts were flooding through my mind and yet I did not show anything to my outside world, keeping fake smiles so that it would not affect anyone around me.

We all gather up with our coach to receive our trophy and pose for the lovely picture which is going to be placed in our college forever. It would be a great memory, and we could see it in the papers tomorrow. We all cheered together and then when I noticed my family, they were all standing up near the audience stairs and looking at me with their smiles.

It was a great surprise to watch my mom, dad and brother all together without any problems and smiling with happiness. The next moment when I see his mom standing alone even though besides my mother and not completely alone, I feel a weight in my chest missing him and his smiling face.

I just waved them and informed my teammates that I would join them later, I ran up to them.

Scott came towards me and hugged me tightly.

"You did it Stella" he busted in happiness.

My mom came next to me "I'm proud of you" she tapped on my shoulders, and I smiled looking at Rob's mom.

My dad was standing a foot behind watching us.

All of a sudden some feeling rushed over me, and I got tears when he extended his hands for a hug.

I ran to him crying in tears and hugged him. He has never been a good father to me from my childhood and now I see a man standing in front of me changed all over just for me. He was neatly dressed and when I hugged him there was no smell of alcohol and just a smell of mint or some chewing gum flavour.

"I'm sorry" he said over my shoulders, still hugging me.

I did not have words to speak, and the tears were flowing just like that which I was not able to control at all.

He pulled me back, watching me in tears he wiped it out

“My little girl should never cry hereon” he said.

Still, I was feeling like I'm in a dream. I pinch him and he bounces moving a bit.

I laugh and say, “Was just checking”.

“I cannot promise you anything, but I would definitely try to become a better man.” he says smiling and the hope in my heart for him has grown.

I turn over to look at my mom and others. All three were smiling at me and looking at my mom I could know that still she is not ready to accept my dad which I'm fine with. She has endured more than any of us has, so she needs time and dad also needs to prove more than this.

“Go pick up your things. Let's leave” she says.

When they all moved and Rob’s mom had a little distance with others, I hold her hand

“Where is he?” I ask her in curiosity.

“Stella” she stammers “I don’t know where he is. I was waiting to talk to you, but did not want to ruin your happiness”

I get serious “There is no happiness without him”

She comes closer to me “I don’t know what happened. When he came back home, he was all normal and we were about to leave. Suddenly he came rushing from his room and went outside slamming the door. Before I could ask anything, he took the car and left” her voice got weak.

“I’ve been trying to get his phone, and he is not picking at all. I thought he might come here anytime but till now It's been more than 4 hours and yet no whereabouts of him” she holds my hand together "I'm so scared and worried. I'm not able to think anything." she says in a concerned tone.

I feel like my world has been stopped and went completely blank hearing all of this. I took a moment to process all of it and came out of it.

"Take everyone home. I will come back with him as soon as possible."

She nods in hope and leaves with them. I stood there for a while watching them go and Joyce came running to me.

"Hey Captain" he hugged me from behind in happiness and I did not react to anything.

He came In Front of me and looking at my face his face turned down "Is everything fine?" he asked in concern.

"I don't know. I should do something. Where he might have been gone. I need to see him" I speak random words and walk here and there looking down and all around.

He kept holding me, making me look straight at him "Stella." he jerked me, and I was about to break my tears.

"Did you see Rob?" I tell him and he looks surprised and answers

"No. Tell me what happened."

"Joyce, I need to find him. Help me" My tears started to flow down.

"Come, let's go pick your things up and will find him".

He kind of dragged me from the field and to the changing room when Kia and Jude came out.

"Kia, take her inside and pack her things up" and when she was about to speak, he said "Don't ask her anything."

Kia did as she was told, and I was standing like a statue next to her. Each time she looked up at me hoping I would speak or tell something. But nothing came from me.

When we came out Ethan was also standing with them. It looked as if he had updated them with the only little information that he was aware of. They do know how much he means to me, so we all left in a hurry and filled ourselves in Ethan's car.

# CHAPTER 17

Rob POV:

Leaving Stella on the ground I reach home. I know I haven't told her about my dad troubling me asking about the job after college and to join with him or with his known perks. I was happy that I got one without his interference, but maybe as she mentioned I should let him know to avoid stress and pressure on both of our sides. So, I make up my mind having these thoughts and went home. Mom was cleaning stuff and noticed me hearing the sound.

"I will be ready in a few minutes" she shouts from the other room.

I went to her "Where is her mom?" I ask.

"She left a few minutes ago. She just wanted to pick a few things before coming to the match."

I was surprised. "Is she coming?"

"Why not Rob?"

"No, I meant she hasn't been to any till now. Especially after the incident." I say slowly.

“Things change Son. Not just only in a bad way, but also in good ones.” Her words gave me positivity.

“I have to tell you one thing” I say, and she turns back looking at me. “Stella’s dad might also be coming to the match.”

She dropped the clothes she was having in hand and turned to look at me in shock.

“Don't worry. He has promised to Scott that he would not create any problem. I hope we can manage.” She still had a worried look. I was not sure how to console her when I myself was not convinced. But I was thinking only of Stella where my mom was thinking for both. I don’t know how it is going to go, after so long years the family is again going to be in the same place and hope it goes well.

“I trust Scott, mom. If he had agreed for his dad to come then surely, we must accept and accompany them." Yes, apart from us their family don’t have anyone else since their father was alcoholic and had more enemies which could not even be counted.

We had always been with them, and their cousins or relatives did not even help or support them, instead they only cursed since they had a love marriage. It was very tough for Stella’s mom.

“Okay. Then let's be quick and reach before anything else happens.” she says and again starts her work a bit faster.

Before I could move, she called me out. “Your dad called again,” she said plainly, and I understood that it was time for me to speak. I just nodded and went to my room.

I decided to inform him first and then explain it to my mom, because I know she would be happy and would be worried of thinking of his reaction of how to make him understand and now she is already stressed up for Stella and Sarah so I can't pile everything on her.

I quickly changed my clothes and skype to my dad. I did not want it to be over a normal call, since it is very important. He picked up after three rings.

“Hey Dad. How are you? Is it a good time to speak?” I asked, looking at the screen and camera, but his video was black. I was not able to hear any voice or video.

Then suddenly his voice came out “Hey Rob. What's up man?” he asked, and his voice seemed to be different like he is doing something simultaneously and this is not the usual tone he speaks to me.

I kind of felt bad to interrupt him in-between his work but it was Saturday evening, and I did not expect him to be doing something or maybe I don’t know his schedule much. Anyway, he doesn't always have much time for family, so I decided this was not to a good time and planned to hang up.

“It's fine dad. We could speak any other time.” I say and then I hear a female voice.

“Honey, there is someone on call” she says a bit loud and the blackness from the screen turns to a lady dressed up in a night dress or something.

My mind went blank. Who she is and what she is doing. My dad came behind in his casual dress and she spoke.

“Hi Rob. How are you?” Does she know me? How. I did not speak anything since I had no idea what to think or speak.

My dad got the phone from her speaking behind “Is it a video?” I knew he was surprised.

Why shouldn't a son call his father in a video? My nerves went high and the anger in me boiled up realising what was happening there.

“Son, listen. I will explain to you. It's not what you think.” he speaks, stammering over watching me in anger. I did not respond, and he remained silent as well. He moved outside the room which I think is the balcony there closing the glass door behind him. There were beach waves sound, and the wind was heavy where I was able to hear the sounds. The sun hit him directly in the face and he struggled to talk again.

“I was about to inform you guys when I came home.” he starts.

I interrupted him “So this is what your business is? This is what is more important than your family?"

“How could you do this to mom? '' I shouted over the screen and in anger I threw my phone which broke into pieces. I sat down on my bed crying so badly.

After a few minutes I hear mom calling me out to check on me hearing the noise.

“Rob is everything all right?” she shouts from down.

I don’t know what I'm going to say to her. I can't break her heart. How could this man do such a thing to my mother who has only loved him and has not even thought of anything else.

He has cheated my mom and God knows how many times.

I walk randomly over the room, and I know she could come up anytime asking me what had happened.

She should not know. She should never know.

Only these words were running over my mind in repetition. I took my car keys and walked down the stairs very fast. Without looking at her or turning to her side I went out slamming the front door. I did things as quickly as possible and left before my mom could catch me up.

I drove the car at speed and did not know where I was going. I was also not able to control my tears and was wiping it as I was driving. I took whatever turns I could see and kept on driving without stopping. Maybe I even would have crossed the city limits, but the only thing going in my mind is that I don't want to stop and keep going.

Go somewhere where I could not feel this pain and I want it to stop. At a point I realised I had reached some hill point and stopped my car to one side. There was a plain ground and at the tip where I could see the view of the city. I haven't been here ever and reaching there I screamed out loud and cried harder breaking down.

Long hours had been gone and I saw the clouds getting dark. I had no idea how long it had been where I was sitting holding my legs tightly and crying so badly. After a while I realised that I had missed Stella's match and all the thoughts flooded in my mind. I check my pocket and realise I don't have a phone to contact anyone. I went near the car and checked the time which was mentioned as evening seven. I was worried about everything my dad has done and the way I have reacted which would have put all my loved ones in trouble and confusion.

I realised the mistake that I had done, did not inform my mom anything and just came blasting out of home. Stella has a match where she had to face her dad and mom being together when I should have been with her, but I did not. Also, it is her final match which means a lot to her and is very special which I have missed. More than all of these, I miss her. Stella, my only friend whom I need so badly to be with me. She is the only person who could console me. I could not think straight and do something mature.

She is the only one who would guide me well and handle all such complicated situations so well.

I miss her, I need to see her. But how will I? I have left her and have not been with her on this special day. Will she understand if I tell my situation? I hope she will. She has to because I'm the one who needs her the most. I'm nothing without her.

I start the engine and drive my way back looking up the signs to reach the city. It took me nearly an hour and I reached our city's main roads. When I found myself at our regular shop, I parked my car in the lot. I was hungry and I checked the car which had a little money in the dashboard. Also, it is our regular spot, and they know me well so I could ask them for help and contact Stella. I did not want anyone else to contact or know about me. I want her to be the first person to see.

The waiter recognised me when I entered and came towards me.

"What happened sir?" he asked in concern. Was my situation looking that bad, I thought for myself.

"I need to call my friend and I don't have anything with me." I show my empty hands with few changes in it.

He understood immediately and said "I'll take the details from the registry and will call her." He showed me to our regular place which was empty for good. He placed a glass of water in front of me.

"Wait here sir." he said and goes back to another waiter informing him something. Then he went back to the entrance and took out some book searching then takes up the phone to call. I'm not sure what he spoke but looking at his reaction it felt he was in serious tone, and he kept the phone.

A little relief went through me. She would be coming here for me; I thought and drank the water. The waiter came to me

“She will be here within an hour. I hope your name is Robinson Richard.” he asks, and I nod.

I don’t want to hear that Un worthy's man name and got irritated with myself for having his surname.

The waiter went inside the kitchen room and the previous waiter whom he had spoken to came out and brought a plate to me. It had French fries and a burger in it. He placed it on my table and went back inside before I could ask him anything. I took the clue and started to eat it since I was so drained.

Stella POV:

The search was so bad, and we splitted up reaching each place in the city where I could think of and in all the places, we couldn’t find him. The thoughts in my mind were running so badly thinking of all the negative scenarios.

“Does he have the habit of going out of town or anywhere special?” Ethan asked.

And my mind could not think of anything to answer, and I was being silent. We were on streets near the game arena where we played paintball once. Kia suggested giving a report if we could not find or contact him since it has been more than five hours but that did not seem a good idea to me. Joyce irritated me by suggesting to search any bars or pubs which he would never do, and I know that for sure. But the scared and worry in me made me think of even the impossibilities but I did not show it out to them and not leaving any hope on Rob.

Breaking our silence, a call came to my phone and it was a new number. It kind of felt like an instinct and I picked up immediately. It was a call from the café which we used to visit regularly, and the speaker was the waiter. This was the first place where I started and did not find him now. I was shocked to hear that Rob was there asking for help to contact me. I assured him I would come soon and hung up the call.

“Let's go to the cafe” I say to them.

“The same one which we have already gone to?” Joyce asked.

I don’t know why he is irritating me so much; I know I haven't been fair to them by not explaining anything till now and yet they have been with me, but that doesn’t mean they could judge him or me. I just nodded and Ethan started the engine. Kia and Jude have been so much support to me consoling me with good things and keeping my spirit up.

By the time we reached the café I saw his car in the parking lot. Ethan slowed down and stopped on the opposite side of the café. I got out immediately and ran looking out at both sides crossing the streets. IT was a riskier job that I did, but I did not care and could hear my friends shouting behind. I wanted to see him and know he is fine, until then nothing is safe for me.

Rushing up through the front door I looked exactly at our regular table and spotted him sitting on the edge of the seat holding the straw rolling inside the empty glass. Without any more thoughts I walked fast to him standing beside him and he looked up at me. The anger was rushing inside me to scold him and beat him as hard as I could, but his face was dull, and his eyes were swollen.

He has cried. A lot. I haven't seen him cry in my entire life. He stood up and pulled me hugging me tighter and started to cry again and more. He was broken and I could not bear to see him like this. The weight on my chest lifted more and I hugged him back trying to console him.

My friends entered and they understood the situation leaving the café without disturbing us. Rob was holding me for a long while crying everything out and we were standing there for more minutes. His tears never seemed to be lessened, so I tried to remove his hands softly and looked at him. He did not face me and was looking at the floor with tears flowing through his eyes all over his face.

What happened to break him so much, I thought and made him sit on the seat and I sat next to him.

“Everything is fine Rob. I’m here with you” I console him as much as I can. I could not give any wrong words without knowing the situation. So, I was careful with what I said.

“No” he cried harder.

His tears broke me more and it was tough for me to bring up all my strength. I could feel the tears running over my face and ignored it. I must concentrate only on him to solve the situation and take him out of this deep sorrow which he is going through.

I hold his shivering hands and he grabs me tighter “We could solve everything. You know it.” I try to calm him down.

“This is not in our hands Stella. There is nothing we could do. Everything is done and over.” his mouth was struggling to speak.

From his mom’s explanation before he left the house, I was not able to take out any details. I pulled him closer and hugged him. I realised there are no words to console him now and first I should make him get relaxed. Later let him speak whenever he feels comfortable to open. I rub my hands over his back, and he gets a bit relaxed where his shivering gets reduced.

For a moment I hold him until he gets completely stable. He rests his face over my chest and is tired for a while. Then what felt like an hour, he looked into my eyes. I know he wanted to speak but he was struggling, and I felt something was holding him.

"You don't have to say anything until you are ready. I'm always there by your side." I say and hold his hands. "But next time come to me and don't go anywhere else" I say like a strict teacher.

"Sorry" he asks and puts his head down again.

I lifted his chin looking back again at me. "It's fine and now I'm with you."

His face comes back to normal and then he looks around.

"Are you hungry?" I ask

"I already had," he replied, showing the empty plates and glass on the table.

"You left me and ate" I acted as if I'm angry.

He looks like I attacked him and found words to speak.

I laugh "Chill. You'll have to repay for this another time."

He smiled and it felt good. I looked around to find the waiter and he came to us. Asking for a bill, I pay for him.

"Thanks" it was wholehearted and was really a great help which he had done. He smiled back and went.
We both stood up and moved outside.

"How did you come here?" he asked at the same moment we stepped outside.

I raised my hand towards them who were standing at the opposite side near their car.

"I have given trouble to many people" he said again going back to his disappointed tone.

Standing next to him I place my hand inside his arm "That's why friends are for" and I leaned my head on his shoulder.

He turned to look at me and smiled “Thank you”.

Even though we have not solved it completely, watching him relax and normal felt good.

“Can you drive?”

“Always” and he gestures towards his car.

I smile, “Let me inform them and come back.” I left his hold and walked slowly towards the other side and this time I was careful.

They four looked at me in a confused state. Kia and Jude came to me.

“Is he fine?”

“Is everything alright?”

They both ask and I smile. “It's good for now”

“What happened?” Ethan asked, standing next to Kia.

“I don’t know. But he was broken and did not stop crying.” I shrugged, “I felt I could talk to him later when it's a good time.” I looked back at him, he was leaning on his car and scratching it with his hand.

“He does seem fine for now,” Jude says, looking at him.

“We haven't seen him like this when we entered, so we thought you both needed space and left from there.” Kia added in an apologising tone.

I hold her “Thank you so much guys for being here tonight. I could have not been stable without you”

“Then why are friends for” Joyce came from behind.

I smiled and gave a group hug to them. Kia and Jude came with open arms and Ethan was normal. Joyce felt a little bit of awkwardness which he always is.

I informed them that I would be going home with Rob and waved them bye to reach their home safely. They inform me to keep updated if anything and leaves.

Rob was standing the whole time there looking at me. I thought he was in his own world while looking earlier, maybe he made us think like he is not noticing us. I kept my smile on looking only at him and went towards him.

“Are they angry with me?” he asked, and I was shocked to know that he does concern their feelings over him.

“No” I respond immediately “They were happy to be there for us”

He pointed at me “For you” he corrected the terms.

Even though it was irritating to have him talk this way it was good to see him coming back to normal so quickly. But a frown on his face was always there, maybe things were still running in his mind and he did not want to show it to me.

He showed behind me “You have dropped your scarf” which I did not realise when it had fallen.

I tried to pick it up and it flew a little bit away from me due to the wind. When I stepped forward again to take it which was on the corner of the road a Sudden flash of light was felt over me and I was not able to see anything, so I hided my face covering, then hearing Rob screaming my name.

# CHAPTER 18

Rob POV:

I informed her to pick up her scarf which looked good on her but had fallen while she was crossing the road and I turned to start my car. Things are always easy and good when she is with me. Out of all the things that are going through in my mind, having her beside me could be compared to nothing better in my life. Even though I was annoyed by her friends' looks on me, I was happy for them to bring her. Did not decide when and how to speak about it to her but had a great hope that she would solve it for me, and I could get rid of this heavy weight.

Thinking about all these thoughts I hear a loud horn behind me and get distracted to turn around. That is when I realised about Stella. She was moving a bit forward, bending down and picking up the scarf. A huge truck came horning over and my instinct shouted moving towards her to pull back. Before anything could be done, she was hit by it and fell a few feet from the road. The truck turned towards the right and hit the wall of the building.

The scene before me felt unreal and I ran towards her shouting. Few people gathered around us and the truck. I held her on my lap holding her head in hand.

"Stella. Look at me" and I was tapping her cheeks.

She looked unconscious and I was looking for the pulse and heartbeat which was steady under my observation. I looked around asking for someone to call the hospital and an elderly aged man was already on the phone.

"I have already called, and the ambulance will be here in a while."

A small relief came to me but looking at her face, who was smiling a few minutes ago and now in this condition broke my heart.

"Please don't leave me Stella." I cry holding her and pray so badly.

Within a few minutes the ambulance arrived, and she was taken to hospital. I joined them and did all the formalities that were instructed to me. She was taken inside and made me wait outside the ICU. After a while a nurse came and handed over her things to me and I found her small purse that we got together having a cute sticker in it.

Thinking of all the memories I cried a lot harder. This day could not have gone worse than this, I thought to myself. Picking up her phone and unlocking it, my hand was shivering not knowing who to call first. I was still not ready to talk to my mom yet, so I decided to call her mom and inform her. She cried over the phone loudly and Scott got the details from me.

I was waiting for nearly an hour watching people going inside and outside where at times few questions were asked to me. Scott, his mom, his dad and my mom came in the hallway one after another and Scott was the first one to reach me.

"What happened?" he asked, and the same question was over everyone's face looking at me.

What would I say? I was being silent not knowing what to speak.

"Did the doctor say anything yet?" her dad asked me, and I nodded a no.

I was scared, scared of everything that was going around me and sat down on the chair when my mom came near me holding my shoulders.

"Don't worry. She will be fine" she tried to console me, but I was screaming inside.

How do you know? You were not there, and I was the one who saw her bleeding. But I felt there was no use in yelling at her and remained silent. Looking at her dad and my mom beside me, everything came into my mind again which was harder to push back. I have to focus on my friend right now and not on my stupid life. I got irritated hearing everyone speaking around me with assuming voices and I stood deciding to move away from that place.

Scott holds my hand "I will come with you" he mentions and joins me without my answer or response.

This small boy is so mature and is in a relaxed state. I was surprised to see him grow and Stella would be proud too. While we were moving out from that place, I saw two police members coming towards us.

"Were you there during the accident" he questioned looking at me and I just nodded in agreement.

"What exactly happened sir?" Scott asked them.

He explained "A truck had lost the hold of the brake and was struggling to stop. At that time this girl was near the footboard which caused the accident. The driver is at the station for enquiry, and we came here to check on her."

That is the moment even I had a clear idea of exactly what had happened. It was none of our mistake and it was meant to happen. But if I had not mentioned the scarf to Stella, it would have been avoided or instead if I had picked it up then I would have been there in peace instead of her. Thinking of my mistake I moved past them and went wiping my tears.

Behind I could hear Scott informing them "The doctors are checking and still we don't have any update"

I reached the filling station and filled the glass drinking more water. I don't know the reason for my action, but I was frustrated and angry with myself. Scott stood beside me and held my hand before I could take another glass.

"You had more than you should have," he said in a sharp tone. "I know you are upset, but apart from that something is bothering you"

For instance I was surprised to see him even more understanding. Who is this guy and I'm not aware of this Scott. I sat on the nearby chair, and he sat next to me, waiting for my explanation. I took a deep breath and explained to him about the scarf thing and my guilt over it in grief.

He holds my shoulders "It's fine. Nobody is responsible for it. You heard what the police said" and after a moment he continued "We should be with her right now. She can't see us like this, and she won't like it either. We are her only support"

I realised he was right and made my mind to come out of it. I sat straight looking at him and hugged him as my tears flowed down. After a while I wiped my face and stood.

"Let's go" I said looking at him.

He smiled and joined me. We were waiting for a long time being nervous and tapping my foot leaning on the wall. Stella's dad was walking back and forth, both of our mom's were sitting next to each other where my mom was holding Sarah who was crying for a long time. Scott was standing next to me leaning over the wall and the two police officers who came were sitting a few metres away from us.

The doctor came out with a few nurses and looked at all of us. Maybe he was thinking about whom to inform. Everyone focused on him, and he looked at her mom and dad understanding them to be her parents and started speaking.

"She is fine and had only a few injuries which have been taken care of" it was a relief for us to hear these words "But her leg is severely injured, and she could not walk for a while. It is not permanent problem; we will suggest few programmes and will give treatment where she would be able to walk properly in three to six months"

And there came the problem. Everyone was shocked to hear it but at the same time was relieved that there wasn't any serious injury.

"Can I go see her?" I asked, breaking everyone's silence.

"She is in sedation now and will be transferred to her room in a while. After that you can" the doctors instruct and move away.

A nurse comes behind "There are few formalities to be taken care of. Kindly check in the reception for the details."

Both of our moms looked at me and then moved towards reception. The police officers who had come enquiries still more with each of us and informed us that they would be coming the next day to get a statement from Stella and get our details.

I and Scott arranged the room for her which was allotted in the hospital and was waiting. After an hour a few came and shifted her where she was still unconscious. Her left leg was lifted in the air and tied up, her head was covered with those white bandages and a few places had scratches and ointments covered.

It was weird and disappointing to see her like this. The nurse instructed a few things and mentioned only one person can stay with the patient and she has been sedated with pain killers, so she won't be awake for a while and has to stay with her every time.

Before anyone could speak, I decided that I'm going to stay by her until she awakes and will never leave by her side.

“I will be with her,” I said abruptly, and everyone looked at me.

My mom understood and decided to take Stella's mom with her to our house and since her father can't be alone in their house Scott decided to be with him. So, everyone checked on me before leaving. I sat next to her, hearing the machine noise and looking only at her. At times the nurses came and checked periodically but I did not move away anywhere from that place. I wanted to be the only person next to her when she wakes up and I can't leave her alone at any cost.

Stella POV:

The world was dark to me, and I had no idea where I was. The last thing I remember was a light flashing and Rob screaming my name, thinking of him I woke up like I was sleeping for years, and the room was dark with some light trying to escape from the window slides. My whole body was in terrible pain where in the left leg it was more. I heard a machine beeping sound and turned to my left to see it and that is when I realised that I was in hospital, and I had met with an accident. I laughed a bit to myself thinking of my situation and then turned to look around.

Rob was sitting to my right and was sleeping placing his hand over my hand with his lovely ruffle hairs. He always looks beautiful to me when he sleeps. I did not know what time it was, so I struggled to shift my body and try something to get up which I was not able to do. During my movements something fell on my left side which created a sound in that silence waking him up.

He looked at me “You are awake. Do you need anything?” he asked in worry and was panicked.

I laughed at his expression, and he was staring at me. Maybe it was not a good time for me to laugh, but still I was not able to control and kept laughing. He looked confused and asked

“What?”

“What? Did you expect me to wake and cry out of pain” I asked him, offended.

His expression changed immediately and came close to me. I know it's his guilty feeling and smiled looking at him.

“No,” he said in a sad tone “I just wanted to be sure that you are fine.”

He asked again “Do you want anything? Shall I call the nurse?”

Maybe he is not sure what to do.

“I’m thirsty. Can I have some water?” I ask him.

He took the bottle placed on the table and came to me handing it. I shrugged, mentioning I can't have it by myself. He looked around the bed and found the button which lifted my upper body in one hand and held me in his other hand placing the bottle down. The pain in my body shifted to my lower part more and I was groaning. He looked at me and stopped.

“It's fine. You can lift a little more” I instruct him until I reach a comfortable position and adjust myself. I was not able to use my left hand since it was connected to the drips which kind of pained a little when moved and the right-hand wrist was wrapped using the band. He opens the bottle and helps me to drink it and then informs me that he would call upon the nurse to check me.

After a while he came with a nurse, and she was beaming a smile.

“How are you feeling now?” she asked in a polite voice.

“Bad” I frown. I always hated going to hospital and having medicines from my childhood so no matter what I will always hate it.

The nurse's face goes confused, maybe I should have appreciated them for saving my life and should have not reacted emotionally like a child.

She then checked something and looked at the file she was having in her hand.

“Are you feeling dizzy or in pain anywhere?” she asked and this time I wanted to be a good, matured girl and answered correctly.

The smile on her face was back “You will have to be under the monitor for the next two days and the doctor will be checking you in a while.”

“But” I opened my mouth and closed immediately knowing I'm about to ask a stupid question.

She did not ask any further and instructed both of us about the medicine routine to both of us leaving the room with her smiling face.

Rob was scanning the paper of medicines which was given by her.

“I will go check on your breakfast. You have a medicine to take after it”

I frowned at him like a child, and he kept aside the paper coming closer to me.

“I know you don’t like it, but I want you to get alright soon.” he took a pause and came closer kissing on my forehead “I can't be without you and could never even imagine it” he says softly and immediately leaves the room without looking or talking anything more.

This gesture of him was very new. We haven't kissed till now even on a friendly note and I was shocked by his action. Then thinking from his side, I was able to understand his emotions. He was already depressed by some reason and later this stupid accident would have broken him. I hope he is not going to his guilty zone, and it would be very tough to bring him out of it.

Then I also tried thinking of the situation reversed and could not even imagine or feel it, so I stopped overthinking and was waiting for him to come as soon as possible. This lonely was killing me more with these pains and this stupid machine beeping. I wish I could turn it off. I was not able to feel anything in my leg and I was relieved that this had happened after our match. I was not even able to enjoy or celebrate my victory.

After a while Rob came inside with a tray of food which I knew would be dull, but he had a burger in it, and I planned to take it from him.

“Don't even think about it” reading my thoughts he answered.

I gave my wicked smile. He took some bowl which I assumed was soup and started to feed me.

“They have advised to start with liquid food at the beginning and after you get discharged you can eat as you wish.”

I got a quick happiness "Will I be discharged today?" I asked him in excitement.

He said "Not a chance. They said they must observe you for at least two days. ``He kept pushing the spoon inside my mouth, not allowing me to talk. Good thing the soup was a bit better.

"You have a severe injury in your leg. Don't you see it? I think it would take even a week for you to get discharged or come out of bed"

I frown in disappointment thinking of the reality he spoke.

"And I will always be with you." he wiped my mouth mentioning those sweet words and caring for me more.

After that he had the burger for him, teasing me and we were talking and laughing which felt good. I also informed him all the things happened in the finals and my dad was not the person to create the problem. He also apologised for not being there with me during that time and explained a few things at his end, but we did not bring up the topic of his reason for disappearance. Many times, I thought of bringing it up, but he was clever in changing it, so I decided not to open it until he himself comes ready to talk about it.

By the time others came I was trying to be back to normal even though the pain and hospital ambience made me uncomfortable.

The doctor came for his regular check-up and informed me of the same words which Rob had mentioned earlier to me. He also gave me a plan schedule for the next five days and he mentioned that he could think of discharge only after that and left the room.

"What would she do for the exams?" asked Scott and I looked at Rob. I know he would have some answer for it which I have to follow as per his instruction.

“Tomorrow I will talk to the Dean and will sort it out. I hope they adjust it according to her since she had gained the cup of finals for the college reputation as captain.” finishing his speech he winks at me. Yes, he does have a good and valid point.

Around evening my friends came to look at me and shared their worries on their part. It was nice to see them getting flowers for me which I taunted them mentioning they had given me exactly the same kind of flowers on the previous evening before the match. Jude and Kia somehow set up the joyful mood in the room and it was great to spend some time with my friends. They also mentioned the party that happened the previous night in Leili's house which we were not able to attend due to Rob’s search mission and I was able to notice that Joyce always had a stiff gesture towards him though the whole of our talks.

The topic of prom pops up and my mind gets upset thinking that I could not attend it and I look at Rob which he did not notice. Then they leave for the day since everyone has to prepare for the exams tomorrow. I look at Rob

“Don't you have to prepare as well?” I ask him. I was upset that he did not get involved in the prom topic but did not show it to him.

“I made Scott bring the books for me” he picked up a bag and showed it.

I thought I could escape from him for a while, and he responded to my thoughts as always.

“You can never escape from me.” he said with a wicked smile.

We had dinner and all left for home. Rob stayed with me again. He took great care of me which I could appreciate, but still, he would always annoy me in his own way.

# CHAPTER 19

The next morning he got ready in the hospital and left for college, replaced by Scott.

“Don't you have school to attend?” I ask him.

He shrugged casually “I had already decided to stay with you guys this week and managed it accordingly. So now I'm here.”

I don’t know why; I was so annoyed to stay in the same place and was much more annoyed being in hospital. It was like a suffocation for me even though everyone in the hospital including the nurse and doctors were very friendly. My mom just visited before going to her office and my dad has left for his town. Regan joined us during my breakfast time helping me for all the needs that were necessary for me. After Rob, she was completely there with me helping out and taking care of me.

Having Scott was a good distraction for me from my pain and annoyance. He explained the game that he is working on which was great and I gave some of the ideas that occurred to me. This would really be helpful for his college. He is not into any sports or other activities, so I pushed him into Art class which could be added with his grades and he is into a youth volunteer program in which he got interested in doing community services.

Rob came back by evening directly from college "How was your day?" he asked.

"Better than yours I guess" I taunt him to keep up my spirits.

He laughs.

"How did you do your exam?"

He just shrugged and took out a form from his bag.

"The dean approved. Once you are discharged and ready to write the exams they will make the arrangements for it, but they need your parents to sign in and I will submit it tomorrow after getting it signed from your mom."

It was good news, but I was worried thinking of losing my opportunity as valedictorian and he speaks my mind.

"If you are able to complete the exams by next week then you will still be the valedictorian" he says smiling.

I beamed in happiness "How do you get into my mind?" I scowl at him, keeping my happy smiling face.

"Oh, did you think of it?" he smirked, and I made a funny face.

He started his routine again by reading for the next day's exam and Scott or his mom would bring things for him to the hospital. He did not leave from here or go to his home the whole week. He was always with me, taking good care and did not even hesitate even for a bit.

The regular check-ups were going on and after five days of the incident they removed my hanging leg and made it convenient placing it on bed. After that the physiotherapist started coming and was doing some treatment regularly.

After a week they started moving me out of my room in a wheelchair which was a relief to me getting out of the room. I also started preparing for my exams to pass the time to keep up my position during the graduation ceremony. The thought of prom kept popping up in my mind but more than that I wanted to concentrate on my exams and speech.

Once I was moved to a wheelchair, I requested college for writing the exams in hospital with an inspection of staff and would continue the exam without a daybreak so that it would be completed by the time given by the dean where I would not be lagging in studies, and I would get results with everyone. After several requests and explanations with the support of my coach, favourite staff and friends, they agreed, and it was decided to write my exams in hospital with each day each staff monitoring me and only Rob's mom would be with us in the same room. We also got the approval from the hospital for the timings where there won't be any clash with the treatments and medicines.

These processes were huge and all the persons who helped me in this really did a great job. It was hard focusing on everything at the same time, but I had to do it. I did not like the thought of not graduating with Rob, and this was a very big thing that I need to do more than other small worries I have.

Rob supported me in everything and managed his exams as well. Scott was there only for a week and later had to go to his town since he could not miss more classes. Whenever Rob has to go to college his mom would accompany me, and I had seen my mom only a few times. Maybe she was busy earning due to all this expense which was also on my list of worries. I decided to complete my course and graduate on time so I could go to work and earn money soon.

The internship which I had applied needed an assignment to be submitted and only after that I could enrol with them, but it was too late to go to a company as internship now since I would be graduating in a week by now and I must focus on getting an actual job though this could be a backup until then.

The whole exams and treatments were all over in this two weeks of time which was like more than a month for me. With all my loved ones' support I successfully completed the tasks without any mess and today was the day of my discharge. Still, I was using wheelchair which was recommended by doctor that my leg is not still cured to balance the weight of my body due to the injury and it would take a month or more to walk in a stick and to walk back completely it would take six months or more, which is half a year and all these depends on how good I follow the treatment.

“I can't even think of it.” I scuff out of frustration.

“Everything would be fine dear. We are happy to have you back” Rob’s mom consoles me and my mom was packing the things from my hospital room.

“Yes, back in one piece especially” Rob taunts me and I try to hit him, which I failed since he moved away easily from me. It made me upset that I was not able to play normal with him and went into my depression mode. He came closer to me.

“You can beat now” he shows his shoulder for me. I looked at him and then started beating him hard and laughed out loudly.

The doctor entered the room with his nurse “Someone seems Delighted to move out from here”

We stopped playing and tried to regain our serious faces.

“If you don’t want to come back here, then follow all the treatments properly”

I nod making a yes statement.

Completing all the paperwork and packing all of the medicines and things we start to leave. I wave goodbye to all the people who have been so helpful to me in the hospital wishing deep inside that I should not come back here again. My mom joined us from the reception, and we reached home in Rob's car. I could still remember the last time I saw this car, and everything felt like it had happened a few months ago.

We reach my home, and they pull my wheelchair. So, this is going to be my companion for the next few months I thought to myself. As we entered through the door loads of water splashed over me and I could hear Scott's voice.

“Welcome home" he popped up the party pooper surrounded by my friends.

It was a warm welcome and I looked all over the house as if I'm entering a new one. There were decorations everywhere with so many balloons and hangings of a few photos that were taken in the past two weeks of me in hospital.

A large cut-out which covers one side of wall was fixed with the wordings

“Welcome Home

In your absence, you were missed

Now that you have returned, though things they are alright

Let us begin living again”

With a phoenix image on one of its sides and my dad was standing in the other corner of the hallway at the entrance of the kitchen and dining hall.

My eyes were dwelling in tears and Scott came to me for a hug followed by my friends. I did not have any idea that these guys would do so much for me, and it was overwhelming for me. Scott handed a small gift box placing it in my hand.

“A sweet gift for my sister" he smiled and kissed my forehead.

I opened it carefully since I don’t like tearing off the wrap and I found a red colour box. I looked at him in excitement and he gestured to open it. I found a silver colour chain having a heart shaped locket in it, it also had an opening where we could place photos on both sides but now it was empty. I loved the gift but looking at the empty part I frowned and looked at him.

“Where are the pictures?” I asked him out of my curiosity.

“You have to decide it” he said and immediately I responded

“It's obviously you and Rob. What else do I need.” I said out loud and then suddenly looked all around me with each one having each expression.

Joyce came smiling up “Yeah it is a known fact” he cheered up the room which was surprising for me of his reaction, and everyone came back to normal.

Scott came to me “It's from my first earning” he told me with a smiling face.

I was shocked. He took the necklace and wore it for me which was apt around my neck and the locket was exactly at my chest. I pulled him for a hug, and he crossed his arms over me from behind.

We five sat together in the hall and Kia kept on speaking about all her things that had happened that day and Jude at times teased her to have a hold of breath, drink water or have something where she might lose her energy by her non-stop talking and others were not found in the room.

She later was telling about her and Ethan's plan for the prom tomorrow and it was going to be their first out officially which was happy for her. My mind ran back to Rob thinking of not being able to attend it due to this inability and made me disappointed. Looking at my face Joyce changed the topic and interfered

"Is your speech for tomorrow ready?" he asked, leaning forward and interrupting her.

"It will be ready when it is time" I say in a normal tone.

Again, Kia starts "Have you even started with it?" she exclaims.

"It is impossible to make your mouth shut" Joyce was a bit rude but then added "How are you managing her man" he looked at Ethan and asked which made us laugh. She hit him where Ethan pulled her and kissed her softly on cheeks.

"I don't have to man. She is my girl" he says proudly, and Joyce rolls his eyes.

We have a few more gossip and chitchat, and when it is about to get dark, they wave goodbye leaving. It suddenly felt like I was left alone in the hall since my family members did not interrupt us other than providing snacks and juice for us.

I was thinking how I would be going to my room since it's upstairs and that I haven't decided or got any dress for tomorrow's graduation. Even though the disappointment of prom came through in-between I tried to think positively that at least I'm happy that I'll be graduating with others despite my situation.

"Is that a smile on your face"

I hear Rob's voice and he pops near me on the sofa. I was thinking of how well it would be if things were normal, and we both would have gone together to prom with my other friends. But now nothing can be done.

"Nothing" I shrugged and looked into my phone.

He was lying comfortably on the sofa and then called me out.

"Could you do me a favour?"

I looked at him irritated. What is he trying to prove by repeatedly mentioning to me that I could not do normal stuff?

Without my response he asks "My phone charger is there in that lower cupboard. Could you take it up and give it up?"

I stared at him.

He acted as if nothing was weird "What? It's not a big deal"

Don't know why, but I still listened to him and rolled the wheels using my hand to reach there. Once I opened it, I found a big box wrapped in a gift cover. With a huge smile I turned and looked at him, he sat straight giving a nod in agreement.

I took up the box which was a bit heavy and placed it on the floor.

"I need some help" I asked him, and he pushed up the small table near me. Still his taunting behaviour would never go away, I thought and smiled to myself.

It was wrapped with a yellow ribbon over a red wrapper. It took a while for me to open it and after I finished I placed the box down on the floor to look inside. There was another box with blue wrapper and took it which was followed by another box inside it with purple wrapper. I was shocked to see two boxes and looked at him once again.

He did not give any clue or say anything, just was sitting there keeping both his hands sideways and looking sharply at me waiting for me to open it. Was he not aware of these and I opened it again in eagerness and found a note placed over a box. Over the note it was written

“Open before you read”

So, I followed the instructions and was amazed looking into it. There was a peach-colored soft material inside it, and I pulled it out to have a full look keeping the note aside to read it later. It was a formal jumpsuit which had a rounded neck with an oval hole at the top and a belt to tighten up at the waist. It looked so classy and modern as well which is perfect for my choice to wear. My whole face lit in happiness, and I took the note reading it.

“To the most strong and proud women of my life. Wear it tomorrow for graduation." And was signed as R. I laughed and looked at him where he was casually sitting after doing this much for me.

“Do you like it?” he asked

“It's perfect” I exclaimed and hugged the dress feeling its material’s softness.

This was a great gift from him, and I beamed in happiness looking at him. He gestured to the box which I forgot had another wrapped box in it.

“Don’t tell me you got matching shoes as well” I teased him.

He smiled and did not answer. I was not able to take my eyes from this dress and moved on as it was hard to. I was scanning it and placing it over me

“Will it fit me? Have you got it the correct size?” I started asking questions at him.

He shrugged and it was weird for him not to talk, so I kept this dress aside and decided to investigate the next box. I shook it thinking I could hear some noise or could get any idea of what it was and ended up finding nothing, but one thing was sure of, this box was bigger than the previous one so I decided that this would be something different.

Once I tore the wrap neatly and opened it, I found another box with another note in it in the same manner as the previous one. I looked confused and this note also had the same instruction to open the box before reading and had a winking face smiley. Out of eager I turned the note and found

"No cheating. First open the box" and I laughed out loud reading it.

So, I kept the note aside and opened the box. Looking at it I got stunned and did not have any words to speak. There was a tissue sheet covered over a black glittering dress and a sheet of paper placed over it. Before I could open the dress, I took the paper to read.

"You have always been so special to me and especially in the past few days, you made me realise how hard it is for me to think of a life without you. Here on I would never and ever break your heart and will try my best to make all your wishes come true and keep you happy. Would you like to go to prom with me?" and it was signed as R.

Tears flowed over my eyes and were dropping on the paper. I heard his husky voice near my ears.

"Would you?" he asked, and I cried more.

He came in front of me waiting for the answer.

"Of course. It's my pleasure" I smile with tears.

He then takes a step back "But only as a token of friendship" he teases me "and nothing more than that"

"Never ever imagine apart from that" I taunt him back and he informs me to look out the dress completely.

I took it out and spread it, stretching my hands and the shine in the dress made it look wonderful. The black net material with its design resembling stars which is shining in silver under the georgette pale colour material present inside gave an outstanding look to the dress. My eyes were twinkling admiring the beauty and I could not imagine myself in this dress.

He does have a great choice and never ceases to amaze me.

“It's wonderful” I opened my mouth astonished.

He gives a smirk smile “It would look awesome on you.”

His voice disrupted me from the magic of the dress “When did you get time to purchase this?" I asked him which was the question running inside me for a long time.

“Yesterday” he finished, and I remember him arriving late which I did not notice much since I was busy in my treatment so that I could escape today from the hospital.

I pulled him holding his hands to me “So finally we are going to Prom” I exclaimed.

He acted like not being interested “Unfortunately, I have no other choice left”

And I hit him with my wheelchair and got disappointed knowing my situation. He sits down equal to me facing directly.

“Nothing else bothers me unless you are always there with me by my side.” he rubs my cheek, making me comfortable.

I have promised him that I will always be by his side and would never break it

“Always.”

# CHAPTER 20

I wake up trying to shift my body which gets difficult, reminding me about my inability in my leg which I still have to get used to. I look at the box which was gifted by Rob and smile thinking this day is going to be one of my best days in spite of all the struggles and worry that has happened in the past few days. Last night was a long one since I was preparing for the speech all by myself even though he was ready to help me out. I felt like I wanted to do it by myself to make me feel like I'm still the same no matter what my physical abilities trouble me.

The paper was next to me under the book which I took once and went through it again so that I could read it confidently on stage. My mom came to take some things since this was her room and has been shifted temporarily for me. She did not occupy my room either and decided to sleep in Rob's house with his mom and my dad and Scott slept in the hall.

They said they did not want to disturb my room and it will always be mine which I felt happy and kind of proud of my family members. My family, wow it was great to think all of us together once again without any problems and we had never been like a normal family. At that moment I think of Rob's dad and ask my mom about him.

"I don't know, but he hasn't arrived yet and Regan did not mention anything about it neither did I ask"

The thought of Rob's disappearance night appeared in my mind again and I was fighting to get answers but I'm not able to know how he is coping without sharing it with me. A kind of jealousy passed over me thinking he found another friend, but it is not possible especially after these wonderful gifts and notes from him. Sooner or later, I decided to talk to him about it and not today.

My mom after a while helps me to the bathroom and gets me ready. She took out the dress that he had given me and appreciated his choice of selection. After I got ready, I looked at myself in the mirror and was admiring.

"You look awesome" Scott entered wearing a formal shirt and jeans tucked in.

"You look like a man" I appreciate him back.

He looks at my sad face and asks, "Why this sadness in this pretty face."

I did not know how to convey it to him, "I wish I could stand and admire myself in this dress." and put my head down.

He immediately looked around him and kept the things he had on the table nearby. Then he came to my left side and asked

"Do you trust me?"

I gave him a confused look.

He instructed me to put my hand over his shoulder and lean my weight on him and I did as he said. He then gripped both my shoulders carrying me halfway where my leg was touching the leg rest on my wheelchair, and he told me to look at the mirror. It was like I'm standing without touching the ground and was able to see the dress as I wished.

I heard a shutter sound click and turned around where Rob was taking a picture of us. Then we gave a quick fun and normal pose making him click more pictures.

“Okay. I’m done. Balance yourself” Scott says as I sit back.

I was overwhelmed by joy and surprised by my brother's mature way of thinking. I look at Rob and speak

“My small boy has grown up” with pride in my voice.

“I realised it already” He then shows us the pictures, and we finish our breakfast leaving for our graduating ceremony where our parents would join us later in a while before a few minutes of starting.

We had to be a bit early to check on everything with the staff and a few final preparations. As we start moving to the auditorium reaching the college Leili comes up.

“How are you doing Stella?” she asked in a concerned voice which was surprising “By the way, lovely dress. It looks good on you.”

It was new to face her complimenting and I did not know what to respond or answer and was just giving her a smile to be polite.

“Okay. See you later. Gotta goes.” she says and hurries to the other side.

I turned to Rob “What was this all about?” I ask him expecting an answer.

“I have no idea. But it's good thing that she is not jealous.” I ignored it since it was not related to my question and looked at my friends who were coming to me in joy.

“Wow. You look beautiful” Kia exclaims and Jude joins with her complimenting.

Ethan holds Kia's hand “It's better if we go quick”

Before I could turn to Rob and inform him, he waves bye and goes in the direction of his allocated seat handing me to Jude. We moved to our places seated for us and as the ceremony was about to start a staff came to us calling me to be on the stage so that it would be easy for the speech to be delivered. Everything was arranged and the function started with each of them speaking including the chief guest.

And now it was my turn to speak where I was nervous and took a glance at Rob’s direction where he looked at me and gave a thumbs up. Building my confidence, I scroll myself towards the centre having a mic in one hand and the speech paper in the other hand.

“THE SPEECH”

*“It's a great honour to speak here on this auspicious day so thank you everyone for that. First, we have much to be thankful for. Here at Langara college we have received a great education thanks to our fine administration and teachers. We are prepared to move on and to take on whatever challenges come next in our lives.*

*We can also be thankful for our families. These past four years have presented us with a lot of ups and downs, and it is good to know that we had our families in our corner, supporting us along the way. Thanks Mom and Dad. I would not be here today without you.*

*Finally, we can be thankful for each other. The friendships that we have made here will last a lifetime. In the same way we have supported each other and helped each other succeed in these years, I hope we will continue to provide support and encouragement for each other in future endeavours.*

*I would not believe it if anyone would have told me last month that I would be on a wheelchair during my valedictorian speech but here I am. We might not know what happens next and anything might happen within a fraction of a minute.*

*You know, I used to think the future was solid or fixed, something you can have control over when you plan it accordingly and work hard or smart for it which I had always done from my childhood. But the fact is it's not. The future is not fixed. It's fluid but where you can enjoy the process in present and be happy for what you are and what you have always been. No one can steal yourself from you.*

*Often on graduation day we look outside for heroes, but I see them right here among us. I have seen in my years here in this college that we don't have to look far for inspiration and that we each have the potential to make an inspiring contribution to others, by being true to our values and committing ourselves to lofty goals.*

*When you leave here today, celebrate what you have accomplished, but look forward with an eye toward how you, too, can be the inspiration for others*

*Enjoy the process of your search without succumbing to the pressure of the result.*

*Thank you."*

Once I'm done everybody stood up and gave a huge applause which was unexpected and when I turned to see my staff on the stage even, they were standing with the chief guest and were applauding. It was really a great and proud moment in my life.

All the other processes were done, and we all had graduated which was a huge moment for everyone. We all gathered at the meeting place with all smiling faces and our parents came towards us. All exchanged a few words and took more and more pictures where at last the usual picture of throwing our caps took place.

I was with Rob and Scott speaking with a few other classmates when Sam came to us.

“It was a great speech, Stella. Congratulations” he informed and was disturbed by something to speak up. After a moment he asked “Are you coming today? To prom” he paused and spoke nervously.

Scott gave a laugh and controlled immediately. Before I could respond Rob answered

“Of course, we would see you in the evening” he says and pats on his shoulder.

Sam did not respond much and waved us bye.

“Pity Sam Parker” laughed Scott and I told him not to tease.

Rob was quite tense, and I held his hand giving him comfort. We all return together to my home, and I move to the room to take some rest after doing some exercise that was to be done. Since I slept late last night the moment I went into the room I decided to take a nap and Scott helped me up and tucked me in.

What felt like just a few minutes for me was actually three hours and Scott was waking me up. He looks up at me

“Wake up Stella, it's time. You must get ready” he searches for something, and Rob’s mom enters the room.

“Hello beauty, it's time to wake up” She holds the box that Rob has gifted me.

Scott waves bye to me informing me that he is going to Rob’s house.

Regan helped me in dressing and make-up which was perfect, and I was completely ready in an hour and at the same moment we heard voices from the hall calling us out, so she took me slowly and everyone gave an awed expression seeing me opening their mouths. Rob was there with his tuxedo put in and was looking handsome. I gave the same expression on seeing him which was vice versa at his end as well. He was having a white rose in his hand and came to me kneeling in front of me giving the flower.

"For the most beautiful lady in the world and my most special person"

I get it softly from him and wink him "Thank you"

He holds my hand out and we pose to click a picture. We waved everyone and he helped me to take a seat in the front seat of the car and placed the chair behind. We drove to the party hall which took us a while and while entering, the pathway was filled with lights and flowers. In the entrance they also took a picture and before we reached it seemed like it had started already which was evident by the loud music.

It was like a dream come true for me to attend the prom and with Rob as I wished for my whole life. There was a huge crowd which felt like more than the graduation place, and few were dancing on the floor already and some were having drinks and food. I spotted my friends who were busy with their own work and just waved looking at me. They were dressed colourful which suited them in their own way.

Rob bends and asks me if I need anything which I nodded, so we take up a table and sit.

"How do you guys even like this?" he asked, looking around at everyone.

“This is what actual teen aged boys and girls like. I think you are old enough to understand it.” and I giggle

He doesn’t notice me teasing him and takes a sip of water while still scanning the room.

“What should we do now?” he asked.

I couldn’t stop smiling. “We could dance if you wish, but I’m sorry, you have got the worst partner.” I dramatically show myself “Maybe you can choose someone else if you wish.”

It’s his first time and I don’t want to make it boring for him. I felt bad for not giving him good company.

He looked straight into me “I choose only you” he said in a serious tone. “Who said we can't dance”

Standing next to me he holds out his hands asking, “Can I have this dance with you?”

I smile and place my hand on his with one hand holding the wheelchair. He also moved the wheelchair using his other hand and we reached into the crowd on the dance floor. Some were looking at us in weird expressions which made me feel awkward and uncomfortable.

The music was a pop song in which he started dancing, throwing out his hands and shaking his legs. I know he is the worst at dancing and started laughing. He held both my hands and moved in a way of dancing encouraging me. I just joined him by showing some steps using my body shake and hands which he followed. After a while some of them joined us and my friends came looking at the attention here and joined with us. It was a different kind of fun having everyone around me and making the same steps for the song played. Then the song changed to a romantic one and everyone got coupled with their partners.

Rob was standing and looking at me gesturing to the couple dancing.

“It's fine. Let's go” I signal him mentioning outside the crowd and we take up a seat at a table. He gives me a bottle of water for him.

The lights, music and the fun we had, Yes today is a memorable day that is to be locked in my heart. We had some food and started to move outside of the hall to reach home. It was almost late at night when we had reached my home and he parked the car.

“I hope you enjoyed the day” He asked, turning towards me.

“I love it, Rob. Thank you so much” I moved forward and hugged him.

He shifted “I wanted to tell you something” and I nodded in agreement listening to him.

“I have got a job in Seattle”

And before he could finish, I got excited “congratulations” I beam in happiness. But his face went sad which I was confused with.

“What happened Rob?” I ask him.

“I’m leaving tomorrow."

End of Part I

Part II

Coming Soon

# ABOUT THE AUTHOR

Vaishnavi.M is a new upcoming Indian author who currently resides in Tamil Nadu. She is an independent woman who values every kind of relationship to each and every person who has been in her life. She has been a bookworm since high school and has pursued her dream of reading several books. Her interest grew as an inspiration to convey her ideas through books in which she wanted to let the world know about the relationships of life.

www.ingramcontent.com/pod-product-compliance
Lightning Source LLC
LaVergne TN
LVHW010551160826
845677LV00013B/3088

* 9 7 8 9 3 5 7 8 0 0 1 0 5 *